BUZZ AROUND THE TRACK

They Said It

"Now that I know Sam is my son, I'm going to do the right thing. I have no intention of walking away from him. I'm going to make him proud of me, I swear it."
—Will Branch

"Once Will Branch was my dream, but I was a girl then, naive and hopeful. I am neither of those now."
—Zoe Hitchens

"I see the way my son Will looks at Zoe. She makes him happy. They might be going through a difficult time now, but I know they'll work things out."
—Maeve Branch Lawrence

"Sure, Alan Cargill and I didn't get along... he accused me of cheating. But I didn't kill him!"
—Brent Sanford

JEAN BRASHEAR

Two-time RITA® Award finalist, *Romantic Times BOOKreviews* Series Storyteller of the Year and recipient of numerous other awards, Jean has always enjoyed the chance to learn something new while doing research for her books—but never has any subject swept her off her feet like NASCAR. Starting out as someone who wondered what could possibly be interesting about cars racing, she's become a die-hard fan, only too happy to tell anyone she meets how fascinating the world of NASCAR is. (For pictures of her racing adventures, visit www.jeanbrashear.com.)

||||||| NASCAR®

BLACK FLAG, WHITE LIES

Jean Brashear

TORONTO • NEW YORK • LONDON
AMSTERDAM • PARIS • SYDNEY • HAMBURG
STOCKHOLM • ATHENS • TOKYO • MILAN • MADRID
PRAGUE • WARSAW • BUDAPEST • AUCKLAND

Recycling programs
for this product may
not exist in your area.

ISBN-13: 978-0-373-18520-7
ISBN-10:   0-373-18520-0

BLACK FLAG, WHITE LIES

Copyright © 2009 by Harlequin Books S.A.

Jean Brashear is acknowledged as the author of this work.

NASCAR® and the NASCAR Library Collection® are registered trademarks of the National Association for Stock Car Auto Racing, Inc.

www.eHarlequin.com

Printed in U.S.A.

To my racing buddy and out-law cousin Jan Brashear—
thanks for being the only one in the family
who doesn't think I've lost my mind!

And to Ercel for switching the channel to the race way more
often than he'd probably prefer to, simply out of love for me.

Acknowledgments

Thanks to Janet Sobey Bubert for clarifying issues regarding
trusts and trustees in Texas. Any errors made or liberties
taken are strictly my own. Thanks also to Ray Mickan for
talking cars and racing with me—and to Danny Mickan, as
well, for keeping my cars in such great shape.

Big-time thanks to my fellow author Wendy Etherington
for always having the answers to NASCAR questions,
as well as being so dadgum much fun to visit!

NASCAR HIDDEN LEGACIES

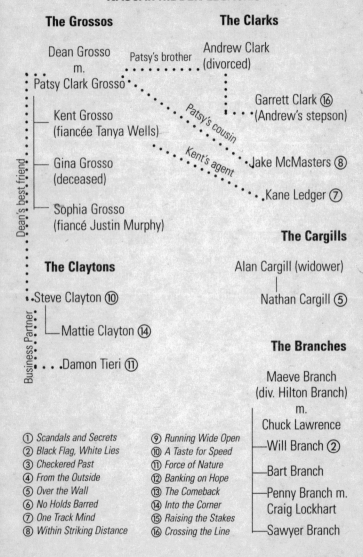

The Grossos

Dean Grosso
m.
Patsy Clark Grosso

Kent Grosso
(fiancée Tanya Wells)

Gina Grosso
(deceased)

Sophia Grosso
(fiancé Justin Murphy)

Patsy's brother

The Clarks

Andrew Clark
(divorced)

Garrett Clark ⑯
(Andrew's stepson)

Patsy's cousin

Jake McMasters ⑧

Kent's agent

Kane Ledger ⑦

Dean's best friend

The Claytons

Steve Clayton ⑩

Mattie Clayton ⑭

Business Partner

Damon Tieri ⑪

The Cargills

Alan Cargill (widower)

Nathan Cargill ⑤

The Branches

Maeve Branch
(div. Hilton Branch)
m.
Chuck Lawrence

Will Branch ②

Bart Branch

Penny Branch m.
Craig Lockhart

Sawyer Branch

① *Scandals and Secrets*
② *Black Flag, White Lies*
③ *Checkered Past*
④ *From the Outside*
⑤ *Over the Wall*
⑥ *No Holds Barred*
⑦ *One Track Mind*
⑧ *Within Striking Distance*
⑨ *Running Wide Open*
⑩ *A Taste for Speed*
⑪ *Force of Nature*
⑫ *Banking on Hope*
⑬ *The Comeback*
⑭ *Into the Corner*
⑮ *Raising the Stakes*
⑯ *Crossing the Line*

THE FAMILIES AND THE CONNECTIONS

The Sanfords

Bobby Sanford
(deceased)
m.
Kath Sanford

— Adam Sanford ①

— Brent Sanford ⑫

— Trey Sanford ⑨

The Hunts

Dan Hunt
m.
Linda (Willard) Hunt
(deceased)

— Ethan Hunt ⑥

— Jared Hunt ⑮

— Hope Hunt ⑫

— Grace Hunt Winters ⑯
(widow of Todd Winters)

The Mathesons

Brady Matheson
(widower)
fiancée Julie-Anne Blake

— Chad Matheson ③

— Zack Matheson ⑬

— Trent Matheson
(fiancée Kelly Greenwood)

The Daltons

Buddy Dalton
m.
Shirley Dalton

— Mallory Dalton ④

— Tara Dalton ①

— Emma-Lea Dalton

CHAPTER ONE

"SMOLDER FOR ME, WILL," the photographer urged.

Will Branch narrowed his eyes. "What the devil does that mean?"

"There!" She snapped several shots. "That works."

Her assistant grinned. "Yeah. Even frowning, he's hot. You could be a model, you know."

He winced. "Not a chance. I'm a race car driver, end of story."

"But female fans love you, and now more of America will, with this fashion magazine spread. You and your twin are going to set some new hearts pounding. Want to see the shots we did of Bart yesterday?"

"No thanks." Will glanced at his watch and groaned. "Tell me we're finished. The NASCAR Awards Banquet starts in an hour. I should never have agreed to sandwich this in."

"Yeah, but you've already got on your tux," the assistant pointed out.

Will glanced down at the bare chest framed by a tuxedo shirt, jeans in place of dress pants. He rolled his eyes.

She grinned unrepentantly. "Well, part of it, anyway."

He returned the grin. He thought about getting her phone number for the next time he was in New York but resisted. He was set for a rock-climbing trip back in Texas right after he got back to Dallas, then he'd go hunting in Virginia with his twin. After Christmas, he'd squeeze in some snowboarding before the whole season began again. Cities weren't his thing, anyway—and he preferred spontaneous companionship over hard and fast plans. Being tied down was also not his thing. He was only thirty; plenty of time to get serious about life later.

He raced from the studio and back to the hotel to change. He'd rather have been getting his picture taken with a championship trophy belonging to him, but after all the chaos of the 2008 season caused by his bastard father, simply making the Chase for the NASCAR Sprint Cup had been monumental—and finishing seventh wasn't chump change.

Next year he'd win it all. No fugitive embezzler father to deal with, no tell-all book by his father's bimbo mistress. No lost sponsors, no devastated mother to comfort. His dad was in jail, the book was old news, he had a sponsor at last—one for whom he had to seriously toe the line—and his mom was now married to a great guy, so Will didn't have to worry about her anymore.

In 2009, he'd concentrate on racing. Period. Even women—however much he did enjoy them—would take a backseat.

He was tying his bow tie and muttering over it when his cell phone rang. He nearly didn't answer, but he glanced at the ID, then frowned.

Zoe Hitchens, his best friend's wife—nearly ex-wife, actually. The woman who'd broken Tanner's heart.

Who'd been Will's girl first—and waited exactly no time before leaping into bed with the best friend he had outside of his brother. She married Tanner and completed the package with a baby.

Though, to be fair, Will had been the one to initiate the separation ten years before. His dad had insisted that he was losing focus, demanded that he get his head on straight to have a chance to move up from NASCAR Whelen All-American Series to a NASCAR Nationwide Series ride— next stop, the holy grail of stock car racing, the NASCAR

Sprint Cup Series. As Hilton had pointed out, Bart was definitely going to make it, and if Will didn't have his priorities right, Bart would leave him behind.

The bond between twins was fierce—but so was the competition. Will had told Zoe they were becoming too serious; she'd only been nineteen and he, twenty-one.

But man, he had trouble getting over her, getting her out of his thoughts—until the day he'd received an urgent message from Zoe and returned the call, only to reach Tanner instead.

Tanner had been the one to inform him that he and Zoe were now together, had been in love for a long time. Planned to get married. What a shock that had been.

Will couldn't say he'd had an easy go of it, but he'd gotten past the blow eventually. He and Tanner, buddies since they were eight, had patched things up a few years later. A long history and being the next thing to brothers had eventually healed the breach.

Somehow Zoe's betrayal hurt much worse, and he had given her wide berth ever since. When he visited Dallas, he and Tanner hung out, but always somewhere else. She'd made Tanner happy—until six months ago, when Zoe abruptly moved out and filed for divorce.

And broke his buddy's heart to bits. Tanner hadn't been the same since, and the divorce would be final soon. Zoe had to know that Will couldn't stand her. So why was she calling him?

Then it hit him that something might have happened to Tanner, and Will grabbed the phone quick. "What?"

Silence greeted him.

"Zoe?" he pushed. "What is it? Tanner okay?"

Her voice, when it came, was heavy. "Will…I don't know how to tell you this."

Somehow he knew it before she said the words. "No."

"Tanner's dead."

"No. I just talked to him—" When was it? Champions Week had been a blur of publicity rounds, photo ops, fans and parties. "Sunday. I talked to him on Sunday." This was Friday.

"I'm sorry." Her voice was tight.

Will closed his eyes. Pictured a boy with red hair and freckles. A man bowed down by misery. "What happened?"

"They're not sure."

No. God, no. Tanner had been despondent when they last spoke, but he was going rock-climbing with Will next week. "This is your fault." Will didn't attempt to keep the bitterness from his tone.

In the silence he heard a sob. He refused to feel sorry for her. She'd been heartless, first with him and now with a man who didn't deserve what she'd done to him. He hoped she suffered. A lot.

He was to blame, too, though. He and Tanner weren't as close as when they'd been kids. Still, Tanner had stuck by him through all the misery with Will's dad. Will should have realized Tanner was in serious trouble. "When's the funeral?"

A pause. "Tomorrow morning."

"Tomorrow? What's the rush? He just—" Will couldn't say the word *died*, not in connection with his friend. "Hell, Zoe, you got what you wanted. You're free of him, so why the hurry to put him in the ground?"

"It's not— He died two days ago, but they're doing an autopsy and it may be weeks before the toxicology—"

"Two days ago?" Will shouted. "And you're just now calling me?" Dallas wasn't across the globe. Why hadn't he heard? Though he could guess: because Tanner wasn't a celebrity, so his death wasn't important to the media. Or to his widow, apparently.

"No one's sure what happened, Will. We're praying it wasn't self-inflicted, but the cause of death isn't obvious yet. Tanner's parents are a wreck," she continued. "And I'm trying to protect Sam. It's all on me, and I'm doing the best I can, but—" Her voice broke. "I knew you'd be like this."

"Like what? Mad as hell that you broke my friend's heart? Made him so miserable that he—"

"Will, please. I thought his parents were going to contact you. I just now found out they hadn't. I knew it was going to be tough on you, and this is a big week for you. I'm sorry."

"The NASCAR Awards Banquet is about to start. I'm supposed to be there." He squeezed his eyes shut. "Never mind. I'll get the first flight out." He glanced again at his watch. He was going to be late, and everyone would already be there, sponsors, his car owner—and he'd barely cemented relations with this new sponsor. Appearances, after all the scandal attached to the Branch name, were crucial; that had been pounded into his head. *No negative publicity, Will,* Sandra Taney, owner of MMG, Will's PR firm and wife of his car owner Gideon Taney, had drilled into him. But how could he go now, knowing that Tanner was dead?

"I know this doesn't give you much time. I didn't pick the schedule for the service. His parents don't seem to care if you make it or not, but I knew you'd take it hard if you weren't here…" Her voice trailed off. "I've been focused on Sam, so I didn't check to be sure… I'm sorry."

Will could not, would not feel sorry for her. But Tanner's son was a different matter. "How is Sam?"

"Not good. Tanner hasn't spent time with him in a long while, but still—"

"And whose fault was that?" Will snapped.

"Will, please— Never mind." Her voice was dull and defeated. "I'm sorry I called and messed up your evening. Please just forget and—"

He was incredulous. "Oh, yeah. I'm going to dance on in there and have myself a great time." He bowed his head and rubbed one temple. "Give me the details, and I'll be there as soon as I can."

In a monotone, Zoe recited the information. Will didn't say goodbye but disconnected with a stab of his finger, then barely resisted hurling his phone at the wall.

He sank to the bed. Dropped his head into his hands.

No one's sure what happened.

Was it his fault? Will wondered. Tanner had said he was fine, that he was looking forward to next week.

He should have known. Should have done something. Though he had no idea what. His phone rang again. He glanced at it. Sandra.

"Hello."

"Where are you?"

"I'm—"

"This isn't funny. Are you trying to lose another sponsor? Taney doesn't deserve this. He stuck his neck out for you, and this behavior is inexcusable."

"I just got some bad news, Sandra. My best friend is dead."

"I don't care if you— What did you say?"

"I have to fly to Dallas, Sandra. Right now. The funeral is in the morning."

"Oh, Will. I'm so sorry. Wait a minute. Let me—" She conducted a side conversation that Will couldn't really hear over the cocktail party chatter surrounding her.

Then she was back, apparently moving away from the crowd. "We'll send you in our plane."

"You're leaving on your honeymoon first thing in the morning. I can't take your plane."

"We'll be fine. I wouldn't mind sleeping in. It's okay, I promise. It will be at least four or five hours before you can take off, though, Taney thinks. All the New York airports are crowded with weekend traffic. He's calling now, though, to get the plane ready. I'll make your excuses. You have to let us know if there's anything else we can do. I'll call Kylie. Do you need me to help you pack?"

His lips curved. Sandra was a combination mother, cheerleader and drill sergeant. She and his PR rep, Kylie Palmer, did a lot for him. "No, I can handle it." *Four or five hours,* he thought. "Sandra, I'm coming on down."

"Will, you don't have to."

"But you're right. A lot of people at Taney Motorsports worked hard to get me through the last year. If this news gets out, it takes the glow off the night for all of them—and we definitely can't risk losing a sponsor, not after how hard you and Taney worked to get Lundgren committed." He rose and smoothed his hair. "Don't tell anyone else. I'll come do my thing and just leave as soon as my part in the program is over."

"You're absolutely right about the sponsors and the team, but we wouldn't ask you to do this. You're expecting a lot of yourself to come and pretend."

It wasn't the way he'd thought this evening would go, that's for sure. But his team had busted their butts for him all year, and Sandra and Taney had backed him through wrecks and stupid moves on the track, through all the upheaval when he was underperforming. "I owe you and Taney more than this. Owe the team. I'll manage, but if you can work out the flight, I'd appreciate it."

"You got it. And anything else you need. Will, I'm so sorry for your loss."

"Thanks. For everything. I'll be down in a minute." He disconnected, considering calling Bart to share the news. Kind of wished he could call his mom, but she was on her honeymoon.

No. His brother had come in fifth in the Chase and would be celebrating tonight, as well. He'd earned it, too—he'd battled all the same problems Will had fought through. And his mother had suffered more than any of her kids.

Will was a grown man, and he would take care of himself.

He finished tying his bow tie and left the room.

CHAPTER TWO

A PARIAH AT HER husband's memorial, Zoe Hitchens stood off to the side, holding her confused and grieving son. Her former in-laws—but they weren't former yet, were they?—occasionally glared at her as they accepted the condolences of their society friends and business acquaintances in the stately, paneled reception hall of the Hitchenses' venerable church. The carpet was so thick that all the talk was muffled murmurs. Soft lighting and strips of stained glass turned one end of the room into a jewel box, but Zoe felt both smothered and frozen. Desperately she glanced toward the one wall of floor-to-ceiling windows looking out onto a manicured garden, wishing for a single touch of sun to warm her.

She'd never been good enough for Tanner's family, and they'd never quit letting her know it. She was sure his mother had been jubilant when Zoe had filed for divorce; his dad had instantly obtained an expensive lawyer who'd opened battle for full custody of Sam.

Sam, whom Tanner had promised to love as his own if she'd marry him.

Only one of the lies he'd told her over ten years.

Like that he'd loved her all the time she'd been with Will—when the truth was that he just wanted to own her. To have what Will had. To outdo his so-called best buddy.

"When can we go, Mom?" asked her nine-year-old son. Tall for his age, skinny as a rail, Sam was serious and shy. Zoe couldn't help but wonder how much of his reserve was due to Tanner's indifference. She tried very hard to surround her son with enough love that he wouldn't suffer, but Sam was far too intelligent not to sense that something was lacking. He constantly sought to earn Tanner's approval, and every time he failed, she could see how it hurt.

That was part of why she'd finally taken the step to leave. It was one thing to live in a loveless marriage herself, another thing altogether to make her child suffer.

I'll never let you go, Zoe, Tanner had yelled at her. *You'll never be shed of me. You're mine forever, do you hear me?*

Divorce was hard enough, but now she was trapped in limbo—not an ex-wife but a widow…putting on a show for the world while fighting off a powerful family who wanted to take her child.

"Soon," she murmured to Sam, wishing she had someone, anyone to entrust him with. She didn't want him here in this poisonous atmosphere, but she had no family of her own, and Tanner had controlled too much of her life, isolated her so that she had no real friends anymore. "I'm sorry, honey. Do you want to go play outside for a while?"

She saw the war on his beloved features. Sam was, in some ways, as much adult as child. He would want to take care of her. "I'm okay." He took her hand, and she wasn't sure who needed the comfort most.

That small action decided it for her. She would not be a woman who would hide behind her child. "Tell you what, I need to talk to a couple of people. You go on out and wait right out there where I can see you—" she pointed to the wall of windows "—and I'll be there in fifteen minutes." She bent her head to his and whispered, "Then we'll sneak off. Would you like to go to White Rock and feed the ducks?"

His blue eyes lit up. Just as quickly, he frowned. "Can we do that?" He was old enough to understand the seriousness of the occasion, but young enough not to know how to deal with his mixed feelings.

"You bet we can." Sam hesitated, and she nudged him. "Go ahead. It's a pretty day out there." At last, Sam complied.

She watched him edge around the perimeter of the room, so typical of him. Sam never made waves, didn't draw attention to himself if possible. He made it outside, but the first thing he did was turn and look for her. She nodded and smiled. Shyly he smiled back.

How she longed to escape with him this second! Zoe forced herself to turn to the room, scanning for the sight of one friendly face. She braced herself to approach Tanner's family, to tell them goodbye as manners would dictate.

Predictably, they gave her the cold shoulder—but with such finesse as not to cause gossip. Appearances were everything with the Hitchens family; God forbid that the slightest hint of scandal should taint the dynasty.

Zoe stood tall and went straight for the source of power: Tanner's severely elegant mother, Louise. "I'm taking Sam home," she said.

One perfectly plucked brow rose. "Oh?"

I don't need her permission, Zoe reminded herself. "He's very upset, and he's too young to be here."

"He's the Hitchens heir. He will assume his father's place in our world."

He'll be part of you over my dead body. Zoe waged the battle of nerves with her look. "His place is with me, Louise. You can't fight for custody now," she said too low for anyone else to hear.

That eyebrow again, mocking her. "We'll see about that."

Inwardly, Zoe cringed, but she fought back for her child's sake. "You're wrong, and I'll prove it to you. Sam will never belong to you." Much of Tanner's problem had stemmed from his loveless childhood, Zoe felt sure.

Just then another mourner walked up, and Louise contented herself with a glare, then gave Zoe her back.

Zoe stepped away, inwardly trembling from the threat, only to stumble over someone's foot. She glanced up to see Tanner's attorney, Howard Faulk. "Sorry."

"Just the woman I wanted to see. We need to talk about Tanner's will. Can we meet later?"

"Does it have to be today?"

"Will Branch is to be there, as well, and he's leaving town in the morning."

Will? So far, Zoe hadn't seen him, and she'd hoped not to. "Why does he need to be there?" But even as she asked, she wasn't completely surprised. It was just like Tanner to issue a *gotcha* to her—and completely in character to include Will in the mix.

"We'll get to that later. Would four o'clock suit you? My office?"

The day had gone from bad to worse. The only person Zoe wanted to see less than Tanner's mother was Will Branch. Better to get it over with, though. "I'll be there." She hoped Sam could stay at a friend's.

"Good." The attorney moved off to speak to someone.

Zoe eased her way through the crowd, jittery to be with Sam, to get away from all the poison in this place. She wished she could scoop Sam up and spirit them both off to another city, another life that very second. She vowed that she would just as soon as she could free herself of Tanner's chains. She was already breathing easier as she neared the edge of the room—

Until she looked out the glass wall and saw her child deep in conversation with the tall, muscular, golden-haired man she'd spent ten years trying to forget.

Will Branch.

Sam's biological father.

"WHERE'S YOUR MOM, cowboy?"

Sam Hitchens looked up, startled, then averted his gaze. "Inside, sir."

"Sir?" Impressive manners. "You may not remember me, but I'm a friend of your dad's." Will started to sit on the ornately carved stone bench beside him but hesitated. "Mind if I join you?"

"No, sir." Then a small smile. "You're Will Branch." He glanced up. "You finished seventh in the Chase, even after the DNF at Homestead."

"I'm impressed." The boy knew the lingo, too—DNF, for Did Not Finish. "I didn't know you followed racing." Will had seen Tanner's boy maybe twice in his life, back when Sam was much younger. He was probably nine now. Tanner always preferred to get together for a boys' night out, *away from the ol' ball and chain,* as he put it. Will had never pictured Zoe being a nagging wife, but people changed. Marriage, he'd learned all too well from his parents, was no guarantee of happiness—more likely, the reverse resulted. He planned to forgo it altogether.

"Oh, yes, sir." He paused. "When your car got loose at Homestead and you flipped over and skidded on the roof, that was really—" His gaze cut to the side. "Were you scared?"

Will chuckled. "I was a little too busy trying to hold on to the wheel to think about how I felt." Then he met the boy's eyes. "But yeah, wrecking is never fun."

"Don't you worry? There's a lot that can go wrong."

The boy sure was serious for a little kid. "We have lots of safety equipment nowadays, and we've all been driving for a long time. Sure, there's risk, but I worry more about getting on the freeway to go home."

"Really?"

"Yep." Will thought for a second. "You think you'd ever like to come to the track?" It was the least he could do for his buddy's boy.

"You mean it?" Sam look thrilled at first, but his animation quickly dimmed. "My mom doesn't like racing."

Tell me about it, Will thought. Zoe hadn't understood the

pull driving exerted on him, and it didn't sound as if she'd changed her mind about the sport. "Your dad followed my career, though. He was my best friend except for my twin brother, did you know that?"

Sam ducked his head. "Uh-huh."

Will hadn't the faintest notion how to deal with kids—not beyond signing autographs, at least. "I'm sorry that he's gone." He hoped saying that didn't make things worse. "I'm going to miss him."

Sam was silent for a long time. He stared at the ground. "He didn't like me much. I don't know why."

Will could not have been more shocked. Sure, Tanner had spoken of his disappointment that Sam wasn't athletic, didn't care much for football, maybe liked to read more than to play outdoors. But Will had never imagined that he'd say as much to the child. Even Will's embezzling liar of a father hadn't done that kind of damage. He'd pushed Will and Bart like crazy, been really intense about their driving, but he had never undercut them.

Come to think of it, though, Will's younger brother Sawyer, a math geek even as a kid, might tell a different story. Their dad's disappointment with Sawyer's lack of athleticism hadn't exactly been a secret.

"Maybe you just misunderstood."

"No," said Sam in an oddly adult voice. "I don't think so—" Suddenly he stood up. "Mom!"

It was the damnedest thing, but Will would almost swear he felt Zoe before he turned and saw her.

Sweet heaven. The sweet, naive nineteen-year-old girl had vanished. A slim, elegant blonde had taken her place. Zoe Lane—Hitchens, he reminded himself—betrayed nothing of her very humble beginnings.

And she was as protective as a mama bear, her arms tightly around the boy she hugged to her side while her gray eyes sparked warning. The air fairly crackled with it.

"Zoe." He nodded a greeting.

"Will." Her expression revealed little, but her face was shadowed with exhaustion. "How was your trip?" she asked stiffly.

So they would be polite. "Fine."

Silence reigned.

"The service was nice," he said.

She shrugged. "His mother planned it."

Another tense silence.

"Well," Will stirred himself, "nice to see you, Sam. That offer stands. We'll be in Texas in April. I'd be glad to show you around."

Sam shifted his gaze between his mother and Will, obviously torn. Poor kid. Left with the ice queen who'd replaced the warm, caring girl he'd once known. Maybe he could look in on the boy now and again—if the child's jailer would let him.

He glanced at her. "I guess I'll see you at four."

If it were possible, she grew even more rigid. "I suppose so." A firing squad would be preferable, that much was obvious.

"Bye, Sam."

"Bye, Mr. Branch."

Will smiled. "You can call me Will." He moved past the ice queen—

Before she gave him double pneumonia.

"CAN I, MOM, please?"

Zoe struggled to emerge from the tangle of emotions she felt being in Will's presence again.

He couldn't stand her. Of all the reactions she'd anticipated over the past decade, the last thing she'd expected was that he'd hate her.

He hated *her*.

After what he'd done, how dare he? She reminded herself that this was an old habit, the pain, the outrage. She understood exactly why he felt as he did. Tanner had deceived both of them. When she'd discovered the extent of Tanner's perfidy six months ago, that's when she'd left him. She'd discovered only days into their marriage that Tanner was insanely jealous and controlling. He'd quickly become a tyrant who used his money and her son to chain her to a lifestyle she hated—but she'd never imagined that he'd engineered everything.

He'd told her that Will didn't want to talk to her, didn't want the baby—wanted her to get an abortion. In turn, he'd concealed from Will that she was pregnant with Will's child, telling Will instead that he and Zoe had been in love even before Will and Zoe stopped dating.

He'd played them neatly against each other.

And both she and Will had bought into it.

"Mom? Can I?"

"May I," she absently corrected. "May you what?"

"Go to the race track with Will in April."

Oh, God. Zoe didn't want to deal with Will Branch, now or in the future. She wanted to curl up in a corner. To sleep for a week.

But Sam was his child. And Sam needed a father who would love him.

Question was: could playboy driver Will Branch be that man?

"We'll see." A very trite response given too easily by parents who really meant no. It didn't require genius to see that Sam could hear that.

"Okay." Her very good, very sweet, very hurt little boy sounded so resigned.

He deserved better. She exerted herself. "It doesn't mean no, Sam. I just can't think about it today, okay?" Tears threatened, and she beat them back.

"It's all right, Mom." Sam hugged her hard, comforting her when it was her job to comfort him.

Zoe crouched to put them at eye level. "I love you, sweetie. We'll get through this, I promise."

Confidence shone in his eyes. "I know we will. I love you, too, Mom." He paused. "Can we still go feed the ducks?"

Zoe glanced at her watch, mentally calculating how close she'd be cutting it. Really close. Probably too close.

Then she looked at the boy who was her world.

The attorney—and Will—could wait. Her child came first.

"Of course we can." She extended her hand.

He took it.

She smiled, and Sam smiled back.

As long as her child could still find even a scrap of happiness on a day like this, Zoe would bear anything she had to.

Even delivering more news Will Branch would not welcome.

CHAPTER THREE

"You're kidding me." Will stared at the attorney. "I'm the trustee for Tanner's estate? Not—" He glanced over at Zoe, who appeared frozen. "Did he change his will after she filed for divorce?" Zoe might be Tanner's widow, but she hadn't meant to be. A few weeks longer, and she'd have been his ex-wife.

"No," the lawyer answered.

"He always meant for me to be in charge?" Will shook his head. "Why would he do that? And what does being a trustee mean? What do I have to do?"

"I don't believe Mr. Hitchens ever anticipated this particular turn of events. I'll be acting as executor, inventorying the estate, filing taxes and such. As for your duties, they will begin once the trust is funded, which is the last part of probating the will. Mrs. Hitchens's household allowance is to continue, but beyond that, only expenditures on Sam's behalf will be allowed, and you'll have to sign off on them." The man cleared his throat. "You'll oversee everything until Sam reaches his majority and comes into his trust."

"Everything?" Another glimpse showed him that Zoe was pale as marble. "I don't even live here anymore. I'm on the road most of the year. Can't this be changed?" What did he care what happened to Tanner's money? Zoe might be cold-hearted when it came to the men in her life, but there was no way Will would believe she'd do anything to harm her child's future.

"Not easily. There were no alternate trustees named in his will, so it will be up to the court to choose one." The attorney hesitated. "Though given the, er, unique circumstances surrounding the marriage, the Hitchens family might choose to fight the will."

"Why? Sam's their grandson, even if—" He noticed that Zoe's knuckles were white, her fingers tightly clenched.

Then Will thought a little more. Tanner's mother had been one of the many in Dallas society who had abandoned Will's mother, Maeve, when the scandal hit early in the year. Even if she didn't feel guilty about that—which she damned well should—Louise Hitchens had never truly approved of Will's friendship with her son. She had a blueblood future in mind for her boy, and though Will's mother's bloodlines were impeccable, his father's sure weren't—even before Hilton shocked and outraged everyone by embezzling millions and fleeing the country.

"Maybe I should let them have at it."

A faint sound of distress escaped Zoe. Such a fate would serve her right, and he felt certain the Hitchenses would cling to their only son's child, give him the life he was born to.

Will frowned. That life hadn't made Tanner happy, though. He'd chafed at it from an early age.

What a mess. He didn't want this, was too exhausted to wade through it. The week had been long and intense, and he hadn't been able to sleep on the plane. He was in no shape to be making decisions. "What if I don't want to accept the responsibility? Can I at least think on it?"

The attorney's brows snapped together. "That's not ideal, Mr. Branch."

"Waiting until tomorrow wouldn't hurt, would it, Howard?" Zoe asked.

The man sighed. "I guess not."

Will relaxed a little. "Thanks. Is that all?"

"For the moment."

Will rose, eager to get out of here. As he turned, he caught a glimpse of Zoe, and a thought struck him. "Will she— Zoe, do you have enough money right now?" He glanced back at the attorney.

"There were no joint accounts, and Mrs. Hitchens brought no separate property into the marriage. Texas is a community property state, but all of Mr. Hitchens's assets were brought into the marriage as separate property, and there was little income created during the marriage. Mrs. Hitchens could sue to claim her portion of that, but it will take time. At the moment, all she has access to is her household allowance, and even that is frozen until the will is probated."

"So you're broke, is that it?" He looked at Zoe, not the man behind the big desk. He did not want to be the trustee, but whatever Zoe had done to Tanner or himself, Will didn't want her starving. "I can loan you some money if—"

He hadn't thought it possible for Zoe to become more rigid, but he was wrong. Her backbone must be pure steel, which fit with the icy woman she'd become.

Then, just for a second, she wavered. Nearly broke. She closed her eyes and gripped her fingers more tightly. "May I—" She swallowed hard. "Will, I need to talk to you."

"Now?"

A short nod. "Please," she managed.

The attorney stood. "I can leave you two here for a minute."

A violent shake of her head. A slant of her eyes toward Will seemed to be…pleading? For a second there, Zoe appeared almost desperate.

Will didn't think much of this woman, but he wasn't a cruel man, least of all to females. He relented. "Finish your meeting with him. I'll wait outside for you."

She bit her lip. "You won't leave?"

Man, she must have some heavy-duty begging in mind. What did she think he was, a monster? Though paying her back some for making his friend's life miserable would certainly be justifiable, penalizing her could mean penalizing Tanner's boy, and Will wouldn't do that.

His jaw clenched. "I said I'd be outside. Not everyone lies, Zoe." *As you have.*

She seemed to get the message and didn't look comforted, but she nodded. "Thank you."

Zoe Hitchens could learn to live with some discomfort, Will thought as he left.

She'd sure caused enough misery herself.

HE LOATHED her.

He was the father of her child.

He wielded total power over the money Tanner had always used to control her.

Zoe could barely hear a word Howard was saying as the drumbeats of chaos roared in her head. She'd eaten little over the last three days. Slept less. Somehow she managed to conclude the meeting and leave with a semblance of dignity, however desperately she wanted to fall apart. She walked down the long hall, yet another bastion of privilege and money, wishing with all her heart that she could simply be alone for as long as it took to gather herself together. To figure out her future. The plan she'd had for life after divorce—finding a job for which she was qualified despite only finishing high school, taking college courses to be able to provide for her son while saving every penny of child support for him…

Everything had changed. She had a little money squirreled away from the tight household allowance Tanner permitted, but Sam, if skinny, was a growing boy. His feet alone seemed to increase every few weeks. There was so much to think about, to worry over, and she was so tired.

Then, at the end of the hall, she saw him. Will.

And everything else vanished.

He hates you, she told herself, *but he was kind to Sam. Build on that.*

But she couldn't seem to still the heart beating double time, the nerves that wouldn't settle. Zoe tried to draw herself straight, to square her shoulders and approach Will with confidence despite the odd flaring of light at the edges of her vision, the narrowing tunnel—

Abruptly, darkness swept over her.

Zoe stumbled—and began falling.

WILL STARED OUT the lobby windows, fists in his pockets. His phone kept vibrating, but he ignored it, unusual for him, given that it was Bart, but this new development had him shaken. How his twin had learned about Tanner, Will wasn't sure, but Bart's persistence made Will certain that was the case. NASCAR was a family, an intimate world where news traveled fast.

Where the hell is she? He wanted to call Bart, but he needed to deal with Zoe first, then get the hell out of here. He turned angrily toward the glass doors leading back to the attorney's office—

Just in time to see her collapse.

He took off running, yelling behind him, "Call for help!" He was the first to reach her, and he barely heard the swell of noise as people tried to help—or wanted to gawk. "Back off!" he snarled, though he wasn't sure why he felt so protective.

Or maybe he did, if he were honest. Seeing her so helpless showed him that he wasn't as immune to Zoe as he'd thought. As he checked for a pulse and found one, relief shuddered through him. He lifted her into his arms, seeing more clearly that her skin was nearly translucent, that she was far too thin, that the shadows beneath her eyes were huge.

"Zoe, wake up. Talk to me. It's Will," he coaxed.

Her eyelids fluttered.

"That's right. Wake up. Tell me you're all right."

"Hey, aren't you Will Branch?" someone asked off to the left. "Look, it's Will Branch, the NASCAR driver. He's one of ours, a Texas boy."

Will ignored the increasing clamor, instead lifting Zoe into his arms, searching for a place to take her away from all this.

"Hey, Will! Over here!"

"Get away!" he snapped. "Can't you see she's hurt?"

The knot of people had the decency to look abashed.

"Sir?"

"What?" Will barked.

A security guard gestured. "Our office is right there. Want to take her inside?"

"Yeah. Sorry." Maybe he could have been less impatient with the crowd, but all he could think was how embarrassed Zoe would be. How worried Sam would be if this made the news. She'd changed in many ways, but she'd been a shy and private girl back when he knew her, and she might be still. Whatever wrongs she'd done, he wasn't taking advantage of her when she was helpless.

Nonetheless, he paused at the door and glanced back. "Hope she's okay," the first guy called out.

"Thank you," Will said, and meant it. He carried her inside.

"There's a cot back here, sir," the guard said.

"Thanks. EMS coming?"

"On their way. You all right here alone? I should get back to my post to wait for EMS."

Zoe was stirring, and some color was returning to her face. Maybe she'd just fainted. "I hope so. I'm no medic."

"Me, either," said the guard. "But you're one hell of a driver."

Will thanked him, then shook his head as the man left. He raked fingers through his hair as he thought about the weird world of celebrity. "Zoe," he urged. "Come back. Talk to me."

She shifted again and rolled her head to the side. Whimpered slightly.

And seemed so fragile. He didn't know what to do, but he clasped her hand. "It's okay. Help is coming."

Her eyes fluttered, closed again just as quickly.

Then popped open. "Will?"

A new surge of relief. "Yeah."

"What—" She glanced at the ceiling, then back at him. Tried to sit up.

"EMS is coming. You just lie still."

Her eyes went wide. "What happened?"

"I think you fainted. When's the last time you ate?"

A small frown. "I don't remember."

"Looks like it's been months." He did some frowning of his own. "You're too skinny."

Surprise flared, then alarm. "Will." She pushed up again, stronger than he'd imagined she could. "We have to talk."

"After they examine you," he insisted.

"No!" She swung her legs over the side. "I don't need a doctor. Please!" She grabbed his forearm. "Please send them away."

"Uh-uh. We can talk about money later."

"It's not about the money." She tried to stand, swayed.

"Sit back down," he snapped.

"Will, I can't. Please. This is important. I'm begging you."

Just then, the door swung open, and two paramedics stepped inside.

"I'm fine," Zoe said.

"She's not," Will responded.

"I just fainted, that's all. I'm okay."

"Ma'am," the taller one said, "we're here and we need to check you over unless you choose to decline medical attention."

"I'm—" she began.

"She's going to sit here," Will interceded, "and let you at least do a basic exam." At her protest, he glared. "For Sam's sake, Zoe. He'll worry. Where is he, anyway?"

It was the one argument she couldn't refuse. With a stubborn tilt of her jaw, she subsided, though her eyes were pure fury. "He's with a friend."

He'd forgotten how hardheaded she could be. Shy, yes, but opinionated all the same. He smiled a little at the memory.

Her shoulders relaxed a fraction. "You won't go?"

His brows rose. "You want me in here while they examine you?"

Her cheeks went red. "No! I mean, you'll wait outside? Please?"

Whatever she had to say, she wasn't giving up until she'd done it. "I have arrangements to make. I'm leaving first thing in the morning."

She looked at the paramedics. "This won't take long, right?"

"Depends upon what we find, but probably not."

"I'll wait, Zoe. Just let them do their job." Will lingered until she relented.

Then walked outside, hoping the crowd had dispersed.

One glance told him otherwise.

"Want me to make them leave?" the security guard asked.

Will shook his head. "Just help me move them out to the sidewalk so she has privacy. Some autographs ought to do the trick." He reached for the Sharpie that a driver was seldom without, but he hadn't anticipated needing one on the day of a funeral.

He'd leave that problem up to the fans. "Okay." He set his shoulders and stepped forward. "Ready if you are."

THE RELEASE was signed, the paramedics were gone, with admonitions to eat right away. The security guard had scrounged up a candy bar and some orange juice. He told her Will was outside, holding the curiosity seekers at bay with autographs. As soon as she was ready, he'd escort her to her car in the parking garage.

She wasn't leaving without Will, though, but where was the right setting to drop a bombshell on the man who was reluctantly playing knight in shining armor for her?

Did it really matter? Was there such an ideal spot?

The guard had offered to let her speak with Will right here. Zoe thought about how hard the discovery of Tanner's betrayal had hit her. The least she could do was to give Will a chance to absorb the news without onlookers. Without having to face other people immediately afterward.

Tanner's house—built to reflect his social standing, it had never felt like her own—was too weighted with memories. That left the small apartment she'd moved to with Sam. It was a risk, gambling that he'd follow, but she thought that plan the most fair. He'd have his own transportation, and she could offer him privacy to deal with the news.

She wrote a note with the address and handed it to the guard. "Would you please give this to Mr. Branch when I'm gone?"

The man looked doubtful. "Are you sure you should be driving?"

She held up the candy bar and took a big bite. Swallowed some juice, though it nearly choked her. "All right?"

"I got a wife about as stubborn as you," he said. "Ought to know better than to argue."

Zoe relished the first moment of true amusement in days. "Thank you. I'm ready if you are."

The man escorted Zoe to her car.

While Zoe prayed Will would, if nothing else, be curious enough to follow her.

HE DIDN'T MAKE IT for over an hour, and she'd almost given up on his coming. For the hundredth time since she'd arrived, she peered out of the blah-beige drapes of the small apartment she'd tried to make homey and was shocked to see him striding toward her.

He cut quite a figure. He was taller than most drivers at six-two, and ten years had filled out his body into what was unmistakably a man's. The rangy boy was now pure muscle and far too handsome for his own good. The golden hair had been cut ruthlessly to control the curls he'd once despaired of, but the cut only emphasized the angles of his face. Eyes as blue as the Caribbean were fringed by thick dark lashes. His mouth was hard now in a face lined by worry, but she could still remember the generous curves of lips that had sent a girl's heart spinning.

Will Branch had been a very hot, very cute guy at twenty-one. Now he was devastating. A male in his prime.

And women loved him, she reminded herself. Plenty of them. This meeting was not about him and her—it was about Sam. She and Will were over and done with.

But Sam had a father he didn't know about. The question was, would Will care? Would he give Sam the love he needed?

Zoe was never letting Sam be hurt by a father figure again. Tanner had done enough damage. Before Zoe would see Will cause Sam one second's grief, she'd disappear with him and start over. She would have to work hard to support him, but at least the Hitchens family would not taint her child's life any more than they had already.

Down, girl, she reminded herself as Will approached the door. *You don't know this man anymore. Be fair and give him a chance.* At the knock, Zoe took a deep breath and placed her hand over her abdomen. Ready or not…

"Hello, Will," she said. "Thank you for coming."

His nod was curt. "Are you all right? Have you eaten?"

"I'm fine. Please, have a seat." She closed the door behind him.

"I think I'll stand. What's this about, Zoe? I told you I can loan you some money."

Zoe watched as he scanned the room, brows lifting as he saw the secondhand furniture. *It's neat, it's clean,* she wanted to argue. *It's ten times better than the trailer I grew up in.*

But she didn't. Instead, she closed her eyes and prayed for courage.

Then she opened them and began. "It's not about money. It's about Sam."

Those blue eyes locked on hers, curious but calm. "What about him?"

She resisted the urge to wring her hands. "Are you sure you won't sit down?"

"Zoe—"

She swallowed. "I've rehearsed and rehearsed, but I still can't figure out—" She stopped herself. Met his gaze. "Sam is your son, Will. Not Tanner's."

He blinked. Frowned. "Say that again."

She rushed to explain. "I tried to tell you as soon as I was sure I was pregnant. That's why I called you when you were on the trip to Canada and left the urgent message."

"But—" A muscle flexed in his jaw. "You…married Tanner. You never told me. You—"

"Tanner lied to both of us, Will, only neither of us knew it. I only found out six months ago."

"I don't believe you. Tanner would never—"

"He admitted it."

"I don't… I can't…" He shook his head as if to clear it. "How did you get this idea?"

"It's not an idea. It's the truth. I saw a message from you to Tanner about our Christmas card. You joked about how Sam looked nothing like him and must resemble me." She clenched her fingers, recalling the sick feeling she'd gotten in her stomach. "The only explanation had to be that you didn't know Sam was yours."

"But how? Why?"

She went on, needing to get this out. "When I confronted him, he…he smirked. Ten years ago, he told me you'd returned my call but refused to speak to me. That you didn't want the baby but would pay for an abortion."

"And you believed him?"

"Why would I have doubted him? All you cared about was racing, Will. I was scared to tell you I was pregnant, but I forced myself to contact you. I hoped that maybe—" Remembering those days, all the heartache, she couldn't continue.

"He was my friend. He wouldn't—" Such pain in his eyes. "Why?"

"You only saw him for a few days at a time. You didn't know him. He—" She fisted her hands. "Back then, he said he'd loved me for years, that I was better off without you. That he'd love me and my baby, that he wanted to marry me. All he asked was that no one ever know Sam wasn't his." She made herself meet Will's disbelieving gaze. "He turned on me almost overnight. Once we were married, he became a tyrant. He controlled every move I made. I could have no friends, couldn't go anywhere without him." She paused. "Now that I know what he did to us and have been around his family, maybe I can understand a little. Tanner never had anyone who truly loved him. He was determined to make sure there was one person who belonged to him, even if—" She fought to steady her voice. "Even if he had to put me in a cage to do it."

"Six months ago, you said. Is that why you filed for divorce?"

"Not the only reason, but yes. The most important one is

that he lied to me about Sam, too. He never loved Sam, and
he hurt my baby over and over—"

"He hurt him?" Rage sparked.

"Not physically, no. I would have left him the first instant,
no matter what it cost me. What he did was more insidious.
Sam never measured up in Tanner's eyes, and Sam knew it."
She couldn't help letting the bitterness escape. "Tanner never
bothered to appreciate that Sam is bright and beautiful, that
he has a huge heart. All Tanner looked at was that Sam isn't
a jock, that he likes to read."

Will looked troubled. "At the church, Sam said, 'My dad
didn't like me much.' I couldn't imagine it."

"I told you, he's very smart and intuitive, as well. And I
won't let you hurt him, either."

Will's eyes fired at her belligerent tone. "Why would I?"
Then he drew a ragged breath. "A child. A…son. I don't
know what to think."

"You don't have to think anything. It's only fair that you
should be told, but I don't expect anything of you."

His brows snapped together. "You think—what? I'll just
walk away? I won't care?"

"Do you?" she challenged. "He doesn't know, and I'm
not telling him."

"You can't do that. He has the right to know."

"Not yet. Maybe never, unless—"

"I have rights, Zoe. You can't decide on your own."

Inside she trembled, but she held firm. "You're not on the
birth certificate. You have no rights."

"I will once there's a DNA test done."

"I have to agree to it. Sam's a minor."

"I could take you to court."

They were practically toe-to-toe now, voices rising.

It was Will, to her surprise, who calmed things down. He
backed off a step, and rubbed his forehead. "Fighting can't
be good for Sam. You have to give me some time to get used

to the news. Thirty minutes ago, I was just a driver. Today I said goodbye to my best friend." He looked up. "Now I'm supposed to accept that my best friend has been lying to me for years. And I'm a dad, when I never intended to be one."

Her heart sank at his words. "Fine. Then just go on with your life."

"I didn't say I don't want Sam. I'll do the right thing." He hesitated. "Whatever that is."

Just as she'd feared. Sam deserved better than another man who only did his duty by him. "You really have no idea, do you?"

"What am I supposed to say, Zoe? What I know about kids wouldn't fill a shot glass. And anyway…"

"What?"

"Nothing. Just, the season is so long, and I travel all the time. I have a lot I have to prove after last year, and—"

"Children don't wait until you have time for them, Will. But you go ahead, let racing be your whole world again. I should never have told you. Just…forget it. Get back to your real life." She didn't know why she was so upset. It wasn't as though she had any reason to expect better of him.

He caught her elbow. "Zoe, damn it. Give me a few minutes, at least. I—" He stared into the distance. "He seems like a good kid." A faint grin flashed. "He loves racing."

"He's a child. He'll grow out of it."

"I never did." Another grin, wider now. "Maybe it's genetic. Hey, he can start with quarter midgets and—"

"You are not sticking my child in a race car."

"He's my child, too."

"Not yet."

He frowned. "What do you mean, not yet?"

"You have to prove yourself first, Will Branch. I am not subjecting Sam to another disinterested father, someone who only pays lip service to caring about him. You can't put a child on the shelf and only take him down to play when you have time."

"But how—" He brushed his hand over his head. "I don't know how this will work."

"Neither do I. It won't be easy. We have separate lives in separate cities. You'll have to come here to visit him, at first. Let him get used to you, and see how you feel about him. There's nothing between you and me anymore, so we wouldn't be one big happy family, anyway. The best I can figure is that you could be sort of an…honorary uncle or something. At least until you stop racing and move back to Dallas."

"Whoa, there. You're getting a little ahead of yourself, aren't you? What if I don't like that plan?"

"You can't tell me you want to actually help raise a child. Do you even own a pet, Will?"

He shrugged. "I travel too much."

"Where do you live? Do you have a proper home?"

He glanced around. "Do you?" His eyes narrowed. "Exactly how did you plan to support him—and yourself? You only finished high school, if I'm not mistaken."

"I'm going to find a job and go to school part-time."

"You don't need a job. There's Tanner's money."

"I was divorcing him. Sam isn't his child, and I don't want anything to do with the Hitchens family or their money."

Will cocked his head. "Do they know?"

"No. I didn't think anyone should hear before you did."

"Man. And I'm supposed to be a trustee and wade through all that mess? Maybe you shouldn't tell them and keep the money for Sam."

"Absolutely not. They've been trying to take Sam away from me. I'm not going to let that happen." She found a brittle smile. "Of course, since they never approved of me and don't like you a whole lot more, when they find out Sam isn't Tanner's blood but yours, they'll probably head for the nearest exit."

"But they'll want to take his money with them."

"I don't care. Money doesn't buy love—or happiness."

"Can't argue that. My old man proved it." He paused. "There's another problem, though."

"What?"

"I don't know how much attention you paid to all the scandal this past year, but I'm on a short leash with my new sponsor and my owner. NASCAR drivers are expected to be reputable individuals. Our fans depend on that. I can't be having any more sordid details associated with my name or I could lose my ride."

"How dare you call Sam a sordid detail!"

"Chill out, Zoe. I wasn't saying that. But the general public doesn't know Sam. All they'd hear is *deadbeat dad* or *illegitimate baby* or God knows what spin the news would take."

"What are you saying?" She could almost literally see his mind racing.

"I don't know yet, exactly. Just that—" He faced her. "We both need time to get used to this, and I agree that we have to be careful of Sam. Maybe we could just ease into this."

"How?"

"Let's keep this to ourselves for a while, as you suggested. It's the off-season, and I had some trips planned, but I'll cancel them. Let Sam and me spend some time together." At her indrawn breath, he held up a palm. "You can be there to supervise if you don't trust me with him. I don't know if I have what it takes to be a father, but I can be his friend. I'll hang around here as much as I can, but I'd like you to bring him to Charlotte, too, and maybe even to some of the testing before the season begins." He grinned. "You might hate it, but he won't."

"He has school."

Will's shoulders slumped. "Oh, yeah." He thought a second. "Some of the drivers' wives homeschool their kids,

I think. I never paid much attention." At her snort, he held up a hand again. "Hey, it wasn't part of my world. But I'll find out. Anyway, travel's educational, too, you know."

"Missing school isn't."

"But a day or two, here and there? Racing happens on the weekends, but testing's during the week. Okay, okay—" He rolled his eyes. "I don't have a foolproof plan, but can you at least give me credit for trying?"

He was right. He'd only just learned he had a child, and he was attempting to frame a solution. "I appreciate it. I…I can't see him hurt again, Will. I won't stand for it. But you do need to know him and he should know you."

"It's the holidays. We have some time to figure things out." He broke into a sudden huge smile.

"What?"

"My mother is going to go absolutely nuts—in a good way. My sister just adopted a little girl, and Mom loves being a grandmother."

"We can't tell her, Will. We can't tell anyone yet, that's what you said."

"I meant the world in general. I'm not lying to my family. We have too much experience with secrets and the damage they can do."

"I'm sorry about what you and your family have been through, but what if you decide this isn't for you? If you walk away from him, that will hurt your mother, too, not just Sam."

"I have no intention of walking away from him, I just—"

"Just what?"

He rubbed his hands over his face, and she could see his exhaustion. "Do we have to have everything figured out right this second?"

She was worn out, too. "I suppose not. But you have to give Howard an answer about being the trustee in the morning."

"Oh man…I forgot. Crap." He straightened. "Look, we're both really tired. Let's just take this one step at a time for now. How about we go get Sam and grab supper somewhere?"

Her nerves were rubbed raw, and she wasn't up to the charade. "I—not tonight. We should sleep on it. *You* should sleep on it, Will." She relented. "You've had a lot thrown at you. This time yesterday, you were on your way to glory."

"Only yesterday?" He glanced out the window. "Seems like a month ago." A vulnerability crept over his features. "I need to understand about Tanner, Zoe. Not right now, I know you're beat, but…man. I thought we were friends."

"He was a complicated man, Will. And he might have—" *Killed himself,* she couldn't finish.

"Yeah." His jaw flexed again. Then he met her eyes. "I blamed you for that."

"I know."

"I'm sorry you had to go through all this. I never intended to hurt you." He shrugged. "My dad was all over me in those days to focus, not to get distracted." A faint smile. "You were one hell of a distraction, honey."

Honey. The word struck a chord deep within, but she couldn't go there. Not now. Not ever. "We were kids. What's done is done."

"Not totally. A child came from it." He closed his eyes. "Wow. I still can't take it in."

She stiffened. "I told you that you don't have to. I'm doing fine on my own."

"As stubborn as ever, huh?" His expression turned serious. "I've got money, Zoe. Not like I once did, no trust fund anymore, but if I can keep from blowing it this year, lay down some steady finishes, make the Chase again and keep my sponsor happy, the money will get better. I'll take care of you and Sam financially, even if I turn out to be a bust as a dad."

"Don't worry about me," she said. "I can take care of myself."

"I'm not saying you can't. But I have a lousy excuse for a father, and though I may not know how to do things right myself, I damn sure know how they get done wrong. Even though I'm a lousy candidate for the white picket fence—"

"Which I'm not asking for," she interjected.

"Point taken. But even so, my boy won't go hungry. I'll make him proud of me, I swear it."

Maybe she'd flirted with the notion of a different response, Will sweeping her into his arms, telling her he still loved her, that he'd missed her. That he wanted to make a family with her and Sam now—but if she had, it had only been for a second and was completely stupid.

Will Branch was a playboy, a hottie, as she'd heard him referred to.

But he was a decent man who was offering to do the best he could by his child. His sense of duty wasn't enough, though, and he could hurt Sam badly if Sam knew he was Will's child and Will didn't stick. She would have to be on guard and walk a fine line.

And be realistic about the gorgeous man who still had the power to move her. If she didn't have a child, maybe she could be tempted by him.

But she would not let herself. Sam was everything.

She would try to just be grateful that Will wanted to do the right thing. Once Will Branch had been her dream, but she'd been a girl then, naive and hopeful.

She was neither of those now.

CHAPTER FOUR

WILL SLID INTO the SUV he and Bart kept at their mom's home in Dallas, but instead of turning the key, he dropped his forehead to the steering wheel for a second.

Holy crap, he was a father! What was he supposed to do about that? How should he feel? For all that he'd tried to stay calm and work things out with Zoe, he felt as if he'd been plucked from Earth and dumped on Jupiter. Or in an alternate universe.

He wasn't one to run to his mother for advice, hadn't in years—but right now, the idea of laying all this in her lap and letting her comfort him as she had when he was a boy didn't sound half-bad.

Which made him realize how lucky Sam was to have Zoe, who would clearly take a bullet for him, just as Will's own mother had always been there for her kids. The thought was a comfort. They'd had a lousy dad, but they'd survived fine because of Maeve. Even if he screwed up with Sam, maybe the boy wouldn't be ruined for life.

Just then, his cell rang again, and this time he gratefully accepted his twin's call. "Hey," he answered.

"What the hell is going on, Will?" Bart was usually the calmer of the two, but he sure didn't sound that way right now. "Why haven't you been answering my calls? Do you have any idea what's going on around here?"

Will slumped against the seat. "I've been a little busy with Tanner's funeral, you know." *And just wait till you hear what else has happened.* He'd give a lot to see the expression on Bart's face.

"Oh, yeah. Sorry about that. Sandra told me." Bart had never really liked Tanner that much.

"Then what are you talking about? I thought you were calling because you'd heard about him."

"Alan Cargill's dead."

"What?" Will blinked. "I'm sorry to hear that, but why are you so worked up?" Cargill, former owner of Dean Grosso's team, was a nice guy, but he wasn't Bart's team owner.

"It wasn't natural causes. Somebody killed him."

"Who would want to kill that old man?"

"The police think it was a mugging gone bad. He was found in a stairwell at the hotel."

"Man, that's terrible."

"Yeah. And you left early."

"So what?"

"So the cops are interviewing everyone, trying to find out if anyone saw something. They wanted to know where you disappeared to, and I couldn't tell them."

"I found out about Tanner right before the banquet. I didn't say anything to you because I didn't want to mess up your fun."

"I appreciate that, but I wish I'd known. It didn't look good that you skipped out."

"Should I call someone on the police force and explain?"

"There was this guy, a Detective Haines. He struck me as the thorough type. I'd guess he'll track you down." He paused. "Or I could call him and pretend to be you."

One benefit of being identical twins was that they'd switched places many times in the past—sometimes with great success but others…not so much. One of the most recent occasions—when a hung-over Bart did an interview for Will, who had food poisoning—had nearly ended Will's career.

"No, thanks," Will responded dryly. "But I appreciate the thought."

"Sandra would have a coronary, anyway." Sandra Taney—back before she'd married his car owner, Gideon Taney—had been ready to strangle both of them for the fiasco. Bart had meant well but, out of character, had lost his temper—on national television, no less.

"Yeah, she might." Will chuckled, though. "I can laugh, now that I have a sponsor, you jerk."

"Hey, most of the time it's me pulling your fat out of the fire."

He was right. Will's temper was legendary. He'd been working hard to master it—no room for missteps now.

He fell silent.

"You okay?" Bart asked. "You sound whacked. What happened to Tanner anyway?"

Oh, boy. "How long have you got?"

"However long you need. I'm not flying home until tomorrow—unless you need me there sooner."

He and Bart fought like any brothers, and neither could stand to let the other win at anything, but when it was time for the bottom line, there was no one Will trusted more. "Looks like there are some questions about the cause of death."

"Whoa."

"That's not all. Apparently, he's been lying to me for years."

Bart said nothing.

"That doesn't surprise you."

"I never understood what you saw in him. He could be a sneaky bastard."

"How come I didn't realize that?" Will shook his head. "Never mind. The point is, you're right, and what he chose to lie about just hit me right between the eyes."

"What are you saying?"

"I have a son."

"What?" Will could picture Bart's eyes bugging. "How—Zoe," Bart concluded, always quick of mind. Then, "*Zoe? Why didn't she let you know?*"

"She tried. Tanner talked to me instead, reported back to her that I didn't want the baby. That I'd insisted on an abortion."

Bart whistled through his teeth. "Would you have?"

"How do I know? I was a kid myself. I have no idea what I would have done, but it doesn't matter. Point is, Sam is nine years old, and I just learned about him."

"Whoa, dude."

"Yeah."

"So what will you do?"

"I just found out maybe an hour ago. I don't have a clue."

"You and Zoe wouldn't…"

"I'd say that's a big *no,* bro. Zoe doesn't think I have the makings of a father, much less a husband." Will paused. "She's probably right. What do I know—what do any of us Branch kids know—about how good fathers behave?"

"Ain't that the truth?" Bart and he were of one mind. Forgiving their dad wasn't on the menu. Out of sight, out of mind was how they'd chosen to deal with Hilton. The old man was in prison and would be so for the rest of his life—and good riddance. Their mother said she'd forgiven him, but she always was the best person Will had ever met.

"She's staying in Dallas?"

"For now. I don't think she can afford to do otherwise. Oh yeah, get this. I'm the trustee of Tanner's estate. I dole out the money to her and Sam."

Bart chuckled. "This isn't funny, I know, but it's completely crazy. Why would Tanner do that?"

"God knows. Plus his family isn't aware that Sam isn't Tanner's. Zoe felt she should tell me first."

"So she was divorcing him, and Sam's not his kid…why

would he leave any of the money to them? Plus, there are the questions surrounding his death. What's going on?"

"No one's sure. They aren't even positive it was suicide."

"Who else knows about this?"

"You, me and Zoe right now."

"Sandra and Kylie will have a cow. Just what you need, more scandal attached to your name."

"Tell me about it."

"What's he like? Sam."

"I barely met him, but he seems like a good kid. Shy but smart."

"He look like us?"

Did he? Will hadn't had time to ponder that yet. "He's got blond hair. Blue eyes. Skinny like we were. Not a jock, Zoe says, prefers to read." Then he grinned. "But he loves NASCAR. Cited my stats for 2008 first thing."

"I like him already. Wow, a nephew. That's going to take some getting used to."

"Sure is. Listen, I'm beat. I hardly slept on the flight, and it's been a long day. Call me when you know your arrival, and I'll pick you up."

"What are you going to do now?"

"Fall face-first on the closest bed."

"Go home. Gerty is there babysitting Mom's dog, Harry. Let her fuss over you." Gerty was their mother's retired housekeeper, but she still visited every day to make sure everyone was okay. Maeve and her new husband Chuck hadn't decided yet where to live, since both owned houses, so Gerty still helped run their childhood home.

"Not a bad idea." They usually stayed with their mom when they were in town, since the house was enormous. "I'll do that. See you tomorrow."

"Sure thing. Oh, and congratulations, Dad. I'll bring cigars."

"Bite me," Will retorted, grinning as he flipped his phone closed.

"WILL BRANCH is coming here?" Sam's voice squeaked the next morning. "How come?"

"He was your father's friend." Zoe winced. Though some friend Tanner turned out to be. "He, uh, he wants to pay us a visit." She straightened a pillow on the sofa, switched it with the one beside it.

"Wow." His little face was shadowed with lack of sleep.

Zoe hadn't been able to sleep last night, either. She'd spent hours worrying over Will, the damage he could do to this precious child. "He'd like to know you better." The look on Sam's face was a mixture of puzzlement and delight.

"Did you decide if I could go to the track with him in April?"

"Would you like to?"

"Yeah!" Then his voice dropped. "But I told him you're not much on racing." Too-wise eyes studied her. "Why not, Mom?"

That was a topic she wasn't about to delve into with a nine-year-old. "I don't hate it, I just—" At that moment there was a knock on the door.

Sam's eyes lit up. "Is that him? I'll get it!" He streaked toward the door before Zoe could figure out what cautions to utter.

She smoothed her hair, straightened the pale lilac sweater she wore over cream slacks. Twisted at the missing set of rings that once graced the fingers of her left hand and stepped from the kitchen.

Will stood framed in the doorway, tall and so handsome he still stole her breath. "Hey there, buddy. Remember me?"

Sam held the door and nodded but didn't speak, shy as ever with anyone but her and probably in awe of the man before him.

"You okay?"

Another nod, but Sam's eyes were on the floor.

"Nice day out there. You like to play ball?"

Sam faltered. Shrugged.

Will Branch had never suffered a moment of hesitation in his life. Couldn't possibly understand a child so unsure of himself. "Is, uh, your mom here?" The two were frozen in an awkward tableau that was a harbinger of all her worst fears.

She moved to intercede. "Good morning, Will. Sam, please close the door."

Her arrival put oddly identical looks of relief on their faces. She froze for a second, seeing for the first time a resemblance between them so strong it rendered her speechless. How had she never noticed it before?

If you hadn't avoided Will for ten years, maybe you would have.

"You okay?" Will asked. "You should sit down. Have you eaten? You don't want to faint again."

"You fainted, Mom?" Anxiety pinched Sam's face. Once again she was aware of how vulnerable he felt, this too-smart child of hers. He knew the two of them were all alone, and he worried over their fate as no child should.

"I'm fine." She glared at Will, then turned to Sam. "It was nothing, sweetie. I just forgot to eat."

"Hey, sport, you got any orange juice around?" At Sam's nod, Will continued, "Would you go pour your mom a glass?" Before Zoe could react, Will had maneuvered her to the sofa and settled her on it.

"Stop this," she whispered furiously. "You're scaring him."

"You're scaring me. You look like hell."

"I can take care of myself," she protested.

"If you get any skinnier, I'm going to have to force-feed you. Don't think I won't."

Zoe blinked. "You have a lot of nerve—"

Just then Sam returned, balancing a glass and focusing hard on not spilling it. Nevertheless, one foot hit the leg of the coffee table, and he stumbled, jostling the glass as juice slopped over the edges.

Will's quick actions saved the day. "Thanks, buddy," he said as he snagged the glass. He wiped his free hand over the outside of the glass before he handed it to her, then glanced around and, finding nothing, swiped his hand on his jeans.

Sam flushed. "Sorry. I can get some paper towels."

Will winked and grinned. "Hey, that's what they make jeans for. A little OJ is nothing compared to transmission fluid."

The glass was sticky in Zoe's fingers, but no way was she doing anything to call attention to it and risk embarrassing her child more. She was grateful for Will's good humor and hoped it would remove the worst of the sting for Sam. He was painfully uncoordinated, his too-big feet always seeming to land in his own way.

"You work on cars yourself?" Sam goggled.

"Not my NASCAR Sprint Cup car. Seth would have a cow if I tried."

"Seth Gallant is his crew chief for the No. 467 car," Sam explained to Zoe. He turned to Will. "What about your NASCAR Nationwide car?"

"I only drive in NASCAR Nationwide part-time, but every once in a while I can get the guys to let me work with them. Mostly, though, it's my dirt car that I work on."

"You have a dirt car? Late Model?" Sam's tone was reverent.

Will looked impressed. "Yep. Race it as often as I can."

"Do you like Late Model or NASCAR Sprint Cup better?"

"What would you choose?"

Sam hesitated. He was a bright boy but careful. Tanner had taught him through hard experience not to open himself up to ridicule. He shrugged. "Probably NASCAR Sprint Cup," he mumbled.

Disappointment chased confusion over Will's features.

He'd been leaning forward, truly engaged, but now he cast a questioning look at her.

There was nothing she could say that wouldn't make Sam more self-conscious. She scrambled to switch the topic. "Did you give Howard his answer?"

Will recoiled. Looked at Sam as if to say, *Should we be discussing this in front of him?*

Of course they shouldn't. "Sweetheart, do you want to have some computer time?"

Sam seemed stung by the dismissal. "I guess." Not his usual response to computer time, for sure, and Zoe cursed her sluggish thought processes yet again. Too little sleep, Will's disturbing presence, the messiness of their situation…all were at fault, but Sam was the one being made to suffer.

To her surprise, Will was the one to make the save. "You like gaming?"

Hope flickered in Sam's eyes. He nodded. "Do you?"

"Hey, am I breathing?" Will grinned. "You should come see the setup I have in my motor home. Plasma screen and everything."

"You do?"

"Oh, yeah, baby. Bart only has an LCD in his." He rolled his eyes.

"I just have a regular TV." Sam wilted.

Zoe was quick to leap to his defense. "Everyone has his preferences."

Both heads swiveled toward her, Will's expression warning her to butt out while Sam's was chagrined.

She wasn't accustomed to being the odd man out. To having Sam side with anyone else.

"Everyone knows plasma is better, Mom," Sam said with just a touch of pity.

Will bent to him. "Girls."

A quick grin chased over Sam's features, and once again,

the resemblance was startling. He shrugged. "Mom's pretty cool for a girl."

Will's eyes flicked to her, and the heated appraisal left her breathless. "Yeah. She is."

This was all new territory for Zoe. The male bonding obviously thrilled her son, so starved for male approval. She wasn't proud of herself that she felt left out.

Her expression must have given away something. "Sam, would you give your mom and me a minute?" Will asked.

Sam glanced back and forth between them uneasily. "I can stay." He took one protective step to her side.

"It's fine," she said, placing one hand on his shoulder. "Your room could use some straightening, anyway."

"Oh, Mom…"

"You heard me, young man." He left, feet dragging.

"What is your problem?" Will asked, keeping his voice low.

"He has to be handled carefully," she said furiously.

"You treat him like a baby. He's nine years old."

She saw red. "Don't you try to tell me how to take care of my son. You know nothing about him."

"How's that going to change if you keep stepping in? You gave me five seconds."

"I won't have him hurt, I told you."

"What the hell is going on, Zoe?"

She blurted out her worst fear. "What happens to him when he doesn't measure up? He's not a jock like you. He's sensitive. Who picks up the pieces when you get tired of him and leave?"

His eyes sparked. "I told you I'd take responsibility."

"How could I possibly count on that?"

"I don't break my word, Zoe."

"You did to me." She wanted to clap a hand over her mouth. She'd had no intention of disinterring the past.

"I was young and stupid then."

"And now you're older and a playboy."

Will's eyes narrowed. "I've done a lot of growing up, especially in the last year. You have no idea who I am."

"That's right," she shot back. "And I can't afford to trust you. Not with my child."

"My child, too." His voice was low but threatening.

"You can't be sure without a test."

He went rigid. "Any fool can see he's mine."

"Biology doesn't make a father. It only makes you a sire. A father has to do a lot more."

"You think I don't know that? Me, of all people?" Then he straightened and took a deep breath. "How can I prove anything to you if you don't give me a chance?"

"Fatherhood is more than discussing video games."

A muscle leaped in his jaw. "That's right. It's also spending time together—"

"Until it's time to go be a driver again?"

"Damn it, Zoe, I'm trying to do the right thing. Get out of the way and let me do it."

"Out of the way? I'm his mother. I'm all he's got."

"No. Not anymore. Now he's got me."

His determined words, his solemn tone sent dread racing through her. "I should never have told you." She started to turn away, but he caught her arm.

"You won't keep him from me or my family. Not now, not ever."

"Is that a threat?" She held firm, though her legs felt as if they'd collapse beneath her.

Will's glare was fierce. "Tanner told me you were a hard woman. Anyone who'd keep a man's child from him—"

"I told you why." Her voice was shaking with anger.

"You've known for six months."

"And what was I supposed to do about Tanner?"

"Why would you care? You left him. You drove him to—"

"Don't you dare blame me for his death." She was doing well enough on her own account.

Will exhaled. Held up his hands. "This is getting way out of control." He stepped away. "I'd better go."

"I think you should."

He cast a glance down the hall where Sam had gone. "I want to tell him goodbye."

"I don't think so."

His eyes narrowed. "Don't push me, Zoe. I have the money to fight you, too."

Fear clawed at her throat. "You wouldn't." Oh, God. This couldn't be happening.

"Mom? Is everything all right?" Sam's voice coming down the hall.

"I'm sorry." Will exhaled sharply, raked one hand through his hair. "I don't want to be at odds with you."

"Mom?"

She stared at Will, heart pounding, and called out to Sam. "Everything's fine, honey. Will was just leaving."

"He's going already?"

Will's eyes remained locked on hers for endless seconds as they both heard Sam's footsteps approach. The atmosphere shimmered with pain and fury, and Zoe was terrified of the future.

"Let's not do this," Will urged, his voice low. "For Sam's sake."

She closed her eyes then. Took a deep breath. What she wanted was to grab Sam, to run far and fast. But when she opened her eyes again, Will's expression was no longer hard but as confused as she felt. "I don't want to, either," she responded.

"I'll call you tomorrow. We'll work something out, okay?"

She nodded, but her chest remained tight. Echoes of Tanner ran a shiver through her. What did she really know of Will, after all?

As Sam entered, Will tore his gaze away at last. Dropped to a crouch in front of Sam. "I wish I could stay, but my brother's coming in today, and I have to pick him up at the airport."

Sam shrugged. "It's okay." But he sounded disappointed.

"Maybe we could all three get together soon," Will suggested. "Bart would like you, too."

She watched Sam's eyes grow wistful at the notion that Will liked him, but he was far too cautious a child to assume anything. Her own eyes stung at the evidence of how much Sam needed a father, how much he craved a man's attention and approval. *You had better not hurt my child, Will Branch. I will make you pay.*

When Sam didn't respond, Will looked uncharacteristically uncertain himself. To his credit, he tried again. "We usually go visit the folks at the speedway when we're in town. Would you like to go with us?"

Sam's whole face bloomed, and Zoe prayed that Will could recognize it. At last, he spoke. "Yeah. If it's not too much trouble."

Will smiled at that. "No trouble at all." He started to rise, then reached out as though he might hug Sam, but awkwardly he hesitated when Sam held back.

Go ahead, she mentally encouraged. *He'd love it. He's just too shy to ask.*

Will didn't finish the motion but instead held up his palm. "Then we will. Give me five."

Sam hesitated, too, and Will nearly dropped his hand.

But at last, Sam proffered his own palm and slapped Will's tentatively.

Zoe held her breath, waiting for Will to correct Sam or deprecate him as Tanner had done far too often. She started to step forward, to intervene.

But before she could, Will smiled at Sam. "It's a deal."

And her precious boy gave Will a shy smile right back.

CHAPTER FIVE

WILL ROLLED OUT of bed for his usual morning workout, but he groaned as he did so. Bart had convinced him to hit Charlie's, their favorite pool hall, to work off some of his frustrations with Zoe by smacking pool balls around.

Pool therapy, Bart called it, with an evil grin. Along with it came a side order of hot women his brother had prescribed to relieve Will of the crappy mood he'd been in last night. Usually either or both would be the perfect cure. Blow off steam, work off some aggravation, have some fun flirting…women and pool and a couple of beers could be counted on to do the trick.

Unfortunately, Zoe and Sam hadn't cooperated. Not that they knew where he was or what he was doing. Or that Zoe cared. No sir, she'd be far more likely to appreciate him disappearing altogether. He wasn't sure why she'd bothered to tell him about Sam when she'd seemed to regret it ever since.

She was the damnedest woman, tying him in knots now as she had back then. Proving to be a huge distraction. He'd barely noticed the bevy of gorgeous girls eager to spend time with him and his twin because Zoe, so fragile and weary, so cantankerous and unreasonable, kept playing tug-of-war with his mind. She drove him nuts at the very same time she touched something in him. She was so alone, and she needed his help, but she was just as likely to slap away any hand he extended.

And then there was Sam. The kid wasn't a lot easier than his mom, in some ways. What the devil did Will know about dealing with kids anyway? Sam was his son—he needed no test to prove that—but he was as different from Will as night from day. Will had no idea how to reach him.

Except racing, which was a sore subject with Sam's mother.

He threw on some shorts, grabbed his shoes and socks and staggered down the stairs toward the gym his dad had installed for him and Bart to use when they visited. Hilton Branch had had a lavish hand with money where appearances were involved. He wanted champion sons, and he would, by God, spend whatever was required to have them.

Will had to wonder how much dirty money had gone into furnishing this gym, but he couldn't bring up such a topic with his mom. She'd finally gotten a chance at happiness with Chuck Lawrence, investor-tycoon and seriously loaded. She'd been on the brink of disaster after Hilton absconded with the funds, and Will and his siblings had resolved to take care of her, even though they'd lost everything, as well. Thanks to Chuck, she no longer needed their help. The best part, though, was that he'd never seen her so happy. So in love.

"Will?" As if he'd conjured her, suddenly there Maeve Branch stood at the foot of the staircase.

"Hey, I thought you weren't coming back until later today."

"I was eager to get back and spend some time with you and Bart before you headed out again. We spent last night at Chuck's," his mother said, opening her arms and smiling wide. "Come here. I need a hug."

"I haven't showered."

"When have I ever quailed at hugging an unwashed son?" She slid her arms around his waist, and Will hugged her back.

"Never," he said, suddenly overcome at his good fortune, having her for a mother. He embraced her harder. "You're the best, Mom, you know that? Have I told you how lucky I am?"

She reared back, scrutinizing him. "Are you okay? What's wrong?"

"Is it so unusual for me to tell you I love you?"

"No. Of course not, no." Her eyes narrowed. "Something is wrong, though. Talk to me. Is it the team? Did your sponsor not pan out? Oh, dear. You couldn't have lost your ride, could you? Not after making the Chase?"

"Mom, Mom—chill." He grinned. She could get so wound up if she thought any of her chicks were hurting. "Racing's fine. My sponsor, well, I have to do great next year, that's for sure, but I have a ride and a sponsor. No sweat."

"Then what is it? Don't try to tell me nothing's amiss. I know you too well."

And she did, he had to admit. He and Bart might fool the rest of the world, but she never once confused them, nor did she ever fail to notice when any of her children were troubled.

"Tell me." All traces of the mother who'd floundered after being deserted and rendered nearly penniless by a cheating husband had vanished. Not the slightest bit of uncertainty remained. For that, Will knew much of the credit went to his mother's own strength but also to the man who had wooed and won her.

"Where's Chuck?"

She spanked him lightly on the arm. "Don't change the subject, young man."

He couldn't help chuckling. "Mom, you're priceless."

She smiled back, but her gaze was still intent. "And if you think that's going to distract me, you're severely wrong."

He sighed. "I need to work out."

"One morning won't kill you. Or you can work out later. Right now, you're coming to the conservatory with me or—" one brow arched "—I'll call in Gerty, too."

Will raised his hands in mock horror. The only thing worse than being grilled by his mother was to have Gerty team up with her. "Gerty's already tried." Fortunately, he and Bart had escaped quickly. At another sharp look, he sighed. "It's complicated."

"Just start from the beginning." She was a head shorter than him, but Will guessed you never got big enough to outweigh your mother's determination. He sure never had.

He gave up and followed her into the room that was her favorite in the house, a lush green space that was spiced with the scent of potting soil and softened by the fragrances of the flowers his mother so loved. She'd created two areas for sitting, one an open spot with a fountain, table and chairs where she would often take her morning coffee—the few times she ever sat still for long.

The other was tucked away in an alcove shaded by an enormous ficus tree. There she'd placed a glider, plump with cushions, that she called her dreaming spot. She led him there, then sat and patted the glider. "Have a seat."

He complied, then stared at a lush plant whose name escaped him, however hard she'd tried to teach him. "Tanner's dead."

"Oh, no! Oh, Will. We hadn't heard." Her hand stroked his arm. "I'm so sorry."

"Yeah." He stared at the tile floor. "Me, too."

"Why didn't you call me? Never mind." She shook her head. "You were protecting me again."

"You were on your honeymoon. You were having fun."

"Fun never comes before my family, honey. What happened?"

"No one is sure, but it appears he might have done it himself."

Maeve's mouth made an O. "Oh, honey—I'm stunned. Poor Louise. She must be beside herself." So typical of his mother that she'd still be kind and thoughtful about the woman who'd abandoned her in her darkest hour. "Was it... Did the divorce have anything to do with it? Oh, poor little Sam. And Zoe must feel—"

"That's the thing, Mom." Will swiveled to face her. "I don't really know how to say this, so I'll just spit it out. I just found out that Sam isn't Tanner's child."

Her brow furrowed. "Oh, my."

"Yeah. But there's more." He took a deep breath. "Apparently, Sam is mine."

Maeve looked as stunned as Will probably had when he'd first heard. She blinked but didn't speak. Grasped his hand. "He's...yours? Are you—"

"Sure?" He started to explain that he had no proof except Zoe's word, but he realized that it didn't matter. "It's like looking at a picture of Bart and me at nine. I have no idea how I never noticed, except Zoe's blond, too, and I've only seen Sam twice in his life and not at all since he was tiny."

And he'd believed his nonfriend Tanner. His non-friend Tanner.

He turned on me almost overnight. Once we were married, he became a tyrant. He never loved Sam. Sam never measured up in Tanner's eyes, and he knew it.

Suddenly he recalled Sam's ducked head, his mumbled certainty that Tanner hadn't liked him.

"A grandson. A boy," his mother marveled. "How could I have missed it? I've seen that child a few times and never once—" Maeve's eyes filled with tears. "When can I see him? Does Bart know? I have to call Penny, Gerty, Sawyer! Chuck! I have to—" She rose quickly. "Come with me, sweetheart." She glowed with excitement. "They'll come for my birthday dinner!"

"Mom." Will hung back. "Slow down. There are problems."

She emerged as if from a dream. "What?" She frowned. "Why?"

"Zoe hasn't told him. I don't think she wants to. And I—Mom, I have to keep my reputation squeaky-clean after Dad."

"You're not going to acknowledge him? William MacGregor Branch, you can't possibly—"

"Whoa, Mom. I never said I wouldn't. I'll take care of him. I told Zoe so. It's just that—"

Her expression turned sad. "You were so crazy about her. I always felt your father was involved in your breakup. Was he?"

"Yeah. He wanted me to forget her...."

She gasped. "She was pregnant then, wasn't she? She married Tanner, but why? Why not you?"

Will marveled that his mom could see straight through to what he'd never considered at the time. "Tanner lied to both of us. He told me they'd been involved while I was with her, and for all these years, she's believed that I didn't want the baby."

It struck him then, all that he'd missed. What had Sam looked like at four, at five? When did he start talking? Did he have a hard time learning to ride a bike, as Will had? Where did he go to school?

Wow. Somehow, talking to his mother about Sam was making the fact that he had a son real for the first time since he'd been told. "I have to sit down."

Maeve examined his face. "Oh, honey. How shocked you must have been." She sat beside him again, then reached over and pulled him into her arms for a hug.

He was so much bigger than her, but for the first time in more years than he could count, he wished he were Sam's size. That he could crawl up on her lap and let her make him believe again that everything would come out right.

Maeve rocked him slowly, and for a moment he let her. "Do you like him, Will?"

Such a simple question. With a complicated answer. "I do, yes, but I'm not sure he likes me."

She drew back. "Why?"

"He's shy, Mom. More like Sawyer, I guess. Really smart, but…Zoe coddles him. I bet he gets the crap beat out of him at school." He went ramrod straight. "I'll teach him to fight. Nobody's going to hurt my boy."

Maeve was grinning at him. "Your boy. Oh, Will, I can't wait."

"You may have to. Zoe can barely tolerate having me around. She's already regretting telling me, I think."

"She's just nervous, honey. And her life has been turned upside down. Sam is grieving over Tanner, and even with the divorce, she probably is, too."

He stared at her. "How do you do that? How can you not even be there and figure stuff out like that?" He paused. "I don't know if Sam is grieving, exactly. Zoe told me that Tanner made him feel ashamed of himself. That Tanner never loved him, even though he promised to."

"That poor child. And poor Zoe." She turned her face to his. "Poor you." She patted his hand. "But you'll be a wonderful father. I've always known that about you."

"Me?" Will's brows rose nearly to his hairline.

"You." She smiled. "Who was it who was always bringing home a bird with a broken wing or a stray dog?"

"I don't know the first thing about kids, and I get mad way too easy. Even if Zoe—" *Wanted me,* he almost said. He went stock-still. Did he want her?

Yeah, he realized. He just might. If he were honest, seeing her again had brought home that there was still something there, however at odds they'd been. He thought of how he'd felt when she fainted, how he'd been ready to do anything to protect her. The notion that he could still care about Zoe after years of viewing her with a jaundiced eye was nearly as big a shock as learning that he had a child.

And foolish thinking, to boot. "Zoe and I stopped being a couple long ago. She doesn't even like me now, and she definitely doesn't trust me. The racing season lasts forty-two weeks, and I'm near Dallas exactly two of those. How on earth can I be any kind of father?" He looked down. "And what would I know about it, anyway, given what mine was like?"

"Sweetheart, you need to forgive your father and move on."

His teeth ground together. "Not a chance in hell."

"You'll never fully get over it until you do." She grasped his chin and made him face her. "And you won't do Sam any good holding a grudge."

"A grudge! I'm not the bastard who ruined your life and the rest of ours. I'm not the cheating embezzler—"

"William MacGregor, stop right now. Get hold of that temper of yours." Her voice was pure steel now. "Look at me. I mean it." Reluctantly he complied. "Do I look unhappy?"

"He nearly destroyed you!"

"I was knocked off my pins, I'll admit that. I'm not proud of how long it took me to get back on my feet. But the key to moving on—besides meeting the love of my life—" at this she grinned "—was forgiving your father and letting go of my anger and hurt. You children must do the same." She met his eyes steadily. "Penny is trying, for the sake of her baby. You have to do it for Sam."

His jaw was locked in place. "I'll take care of Sam, but not that way. He doesn't need Hilton and neither do I."

"Oh, honey." Maeve sighed. "You are so wrong. Your father made terrible mistakes, but he's still your father. How can Sam ever trust you to keep loving him if you can stop loving your own parent?"

Will rose to pace. "It's different, that's all. No comparison."

"Does that thick skull of yours ever get too heavy to

carry around?" Maeve shook her head as she approached. "All right. We won't discuss it any more for now." She smiled fondly. "Let's think of lovelier things, like how it's going to be to have little Sam with us for my birthday. And Zoe, I always liked her." She clapped her hands in glee. "I cannot wait!" She was already halfway out of the room, gesturing him to follow. "Chop-chop, young man. Let's get to work."

Will lingered and watched his mother, who believed that love would solve every problem in the world, race off to tell Chuck and God knows who else—

Oh, man. He'd promised Zoe not to tell anyone but family. Finding out he hadn't kept his word would be another nail in his coffin.

"Mom, wait!" He charged from the solarium to stop her from getting him into more trouble with Zoe than he already was.

SHE WASN'T ANSWERING her phone. He didn't have her cell number. Will entered the Dallas North Tollway on his way to Zoe's apartment.

She probably had caller ID and just wouldn't answer because it was him. They hadn't exactly parted on the best of terms.

So he'd show up. Wait as long as it took, even though his store of patience was minuscule at best.

Though he did hold the trump card. He'd spoken with the attorney earlier and asked more questions about being the trustee. He could hold money over Zoe's head—

But he didn't want to.

He controlled every move I made.

Zoe's life had been tough enough, the child of a single mother who had done her best to support her daughter with minimal education or job skills. He'd met Zoe at the mall where she'd worked in high school. He'd been back in town on a college break, hanging out with Bart and some of his private school friends, killing time on a rare weekend when he wasn't racing.

He'd noticed her instantly. Made a fool of himself, he was sure now, as she worked the perfume counter, asking her to spray first this scent, then that one on herself and taking advantage of the opportunity to sniff her skin several times, to hold her delicate wrist under the pretense of buying his mother a gift.

He'd had no idea what perfume his mom wore, what she'd like. And he'd taken a boatload of grief from Bart and Tanner over the instant crush he'd developed.

Remembering that first day, Will could feel again the draw Zoe had exerted on him. She was beautiful, yes, but it was something else about her that had called to him, though he'd never stopped back then to consider what it might be. He just knew that he wanted her and, like the spoiled kid he'd been, he assumed he could have her. Everything in his life had come easily back then.

Will chuckled at the memory. Zoe had been anything but easy. She'd given him such a hard time that he'd taken to sneaking away from his friends and even his brother—along with their razzing—that next summer, to see her at work, which was the only place she couldn't get away from him.

Zoe had run him ragged, and he'd often questioned why he persisted. He'd chafed at the distance from the University of Texas at Austin—his mother's demand that he and Bart go to college was the one time she'd bucked his father's overbearing ways—while racing part-time. And seeing Zoe every chance he got.

Which hadn't been often enough, but over time, he'd made inroads with her. Discovered that she wasn't distant but actually shy, that she didn't want him to see her real life, where she lived in a trailer in De Soto, a small town south of Dallas.

That she was sweet and cautious and serious—but kissed like a dream, even if she wouldn't let him go all the way.

And that he loved her enough not to keep asking, however miserable that made him.

Until the day she'd stunned him by saying she was ready. He'd insisted that his parents bring her to his and Bart's graduation from college, and he wondered now, thinking back on his father's clear disapproval, how rough that three-hour trip must have been, however kindly his mother would have treated her.

He was impressed, actually, that she'd come. She'd staunchly avoided meeting his family, uncomfortable, he knew, at the disparities between them socially and financially. She'd never let him buy her expensive gifts and, when he'd tried, had insisted he return them.

She had, though, kept a heart-shaped locket he'd won for her at a carnival. It had probably turned green by now, as it was so cheaply made, but she wore it all the time back then.

She'd worn it that night in his apartment, where he'd threatened Bart and Tanner with their lives if they didn't leave him and Zoe alone. He was departing the next day to fully join the racing circuit in the NASCAR Whelen All-American Series and already knew he'd be missing her like crazy as he traveled.

He'd been aware that he was her first, and he'd been scared to death that night. Though he'd wanted her badly, he'd taken the proper precautions to protect her.

Or at least, he'd thought he had. Obviously nothing is foolproof.

He'd never had a sweeter night, before or since. He'd been with other women, but his one night with Zoe still blazed bright in his memory, the softness of her ivory skin, the gleam of long limbs and delicate curves. Her surprising turn from shy and uncertain to fiery as her inhibitions peeled away under his touch.

He hadn't been much of a lover back then, he was sure, but he'd been so crazy about her. He'd never again felt that piercing ache, that need to draw a woman close as though to absorb her.

Zoe had wept that night, and he damn near cried himself the next morning when it came time for them to part.

He'd tried to keep in touch, but Zoe hadn't met him halfway. When his performance had been affected by his preoccupation with her, his father had threatened to pull his money, to end Will's career in racing right there. Will had been torn between a girl who seemed to regret taking that last step—at least that's how he interpreted her increasing aloofness—and the probable loss of racing, a huge part of his life long before he'd met Zoe.

He'd talked to her cross-country and told her that he needed to take a break. She hadn't seemed troubled by it.

He wasn't sure now exactly how many days later it had been that he'd gotten a message to call her and reached Tanner instead. Tanner, who'd always thought Zoe was hot, who'd offered more than once to take her when Will got tired of her.

Tanner had taken the call meant for Zoe, explaining that Zoe and he had been spending time together that summer—a lot of time—in Will's absence.

And had fallen madly in love. Were about to get married.

Will gripped the steering wheel tightly as he remembered his shock, his fury. How he'd slammed the phone down and driven like a wild man that night—and won a big race. His revenge on Zoe for her betrayal.

Tanner, you bastard. Look what you did to us.

What a muddled past. Such a murky future. Zoe didn't trust him, and there had been a lot of hurt piled on to form a brick wall between them.

And now there was a child thrown into the mix.

Racing, for all its complexity and danger, was far more

simple than human relations would ever be. For a second, Will was tempted to turn around, forget about invitations and obligations and uncertainties. Just write Zoe a check each month and send Sam great presents for birthdays and holidays. See him when he was in town.

Pretty much what his father had done, except for trying to control every second of his racing life.

Which was exactly why Will would do the opposite. How on earth he'd manage his career and his child when the child's mother could barely stand the sight of him, he didn't know.

But Will Branch did not shy from risks. Never had, never would.

He turned at Zoe's street and drove on.

CHAPTER SIX

ZOE HEADED HOME, discouraged after a fruitless job interview. She'd hoped not to have to return to retail, her only job experience, because the hours were too unpredictable. Sam thought he was too old for a babysitter, but there was no way in the world she was letting him come home alone after school and remain there until closing time at a mall store.

She'd done it herself, of course—the child of a single parent often had to. But she'd lived in De Soto, not Dallas. Neighbors knew each other; she and her mom lived in the same trailer park for eleven years. Her mother had done shift work for the extra money, most often the three-to-eleven, so by Sam's age, Zoe was coming home by herself, doing her homework, heating up whatever her mother had prepared before going to work, and soon she had learned to cook herself.

It hadn't dawned on her back then that Mrs. Anderson, the elderly lady next door, had spent a lot of time outside in good weather and often invited Zoe over or dropped in when the weather was bad, or that Kim Sanders, the mom across the street, would invite Zoe over to play and stay for supper, all because they understood the struggle that Zoe's mom faced. Childcare would have eaten up most of her salary. In return, Zoe's mom had driven Mrs. Anderson to doctors' appointments or gone to the grocery store when Kim's kids were sick.

And when Zoe's mom died at the hands of a drunk driver in Zoe's senior year of high school, leaving her with no family at all, the neighbors gathered round to make sure she could stay where she was known. Zoe had turned eighteen, so there was no legal reason she couldn't live on her own. The trailer was long since paid for, and a small insurance policy her mother had taken out gave Zoe enough that, if spent wisely, would augment her earnings at the mall and cover the bills until Zoe left for college.

Except that a month after losing her mother, she'd met Will. Will's friend Tanner.

All her plans had been derailed.

But she wasn't going to think about Will Branch now. She had too much else to figure out. She needed a job, and soon, because she'd decided that she had to tell the Hitchenses about Sam right away. She wasn't going to count on a single promise Will had made, but confronting him had made her realize that despite her best intentions, she'd been dreaming again. Will wasn't going to be her knight in shining armor and slay all her dragons. Solving her problems was up to her. There was no reason to delay going on with the future she'd been planning before Tanner died.

She could choose an easier path, yes. The Hitchens family thought of Sam as theirs, and even though they'd never liked Zoe, they would take care of him, would wrap him in their privileged world as the son of their lost child.

And most likely harm him as they had Tanner.

Telling them the truth would set Sam and her free. Free to starve, free to be scared half to death as her mother must have been all of Zoe's life. Never had she understood better what her mother had faced than when she'd had her own child and realized that she was trapped in a marriage that was killing her by inches. She'd wanted better for Sam than the constant fear, and she'd thought that Tanner would come to love him, that the physical security he gave them was better than what Sam would face as the child of a woman with only a high school education.

But here they were, in that same situation, anyway.

Maybe Will would come through as a parent, or maybe he wouldn't. Bottom line, it was up to her to secure their future.

If only she could believe she could make the bright, safe, hopeful future that Sam deserved.

She pulled into the parking lot of the shabby apartment complex she'd chosen after studying the neighborhood crime statistics. It was the best she could afford, though it was far from what they'd had in Tanner's privileged world. It was still a big step up from where she'd lived, even if her neighbors were transient and she was lonely. It would have to do.

Zoe's head sank to rest on the steering wheel. She was too weary and dispirited to move.

But it was nearly time for Sam to get home on the bus. She didn't have the luxury of self-pity. She grabbed her purse from the passenger seat, reached for the door handle—

And stifled a scream as a large form blocked her.

"Hey, easy there," Will said. "I'm sorry. I called your name. I didn't mean to scare you." He tried to open the door for her, but she had it gripped in one white-knuckled hand. He grasped the edge of it and eased it open, crouching before her. Filling up the space with his presence. He reached for her hand. "Are you all right?"

She gathered her wits and tried to still her racing heart. It was as though her thoughts had conjured him. "What are you doing here?" She pulled at his grip, but he didn't let go.

Instead, he drew her to her feet. "I'd say I was in the neighborhood, but there's no point in lying. Where's Sam?"

"In school, of course."

"Oh." He looked abashed. "Guess I'm out of touch with all that, huh? My season is out, and I feel like everyone should be on holiday."

He still hadn't let go, but this time when she tugged, he released her. She bit back any remarks about how all-consuming racing was. "He'll get out of school soon for the Christmas holidays."

"Great. Will you have dinner with my family tomorrow night? It's my mom's birthday and my whole family will be there."

She scrambled for an excuse. "We…we're supposed to be with Tanner's parents." However much she dreaded it.

"The family who wants to take Sam away from you?" He stared at her. "The people who will never forgive you when they find out he's not Tanner's."

"They won't…they can't find out yet." She wasn't remotely ready for the confrontation. Needed to figure out the right time to tell them.

"You can't keep this a secret forever."

"I know." *Blast you, Tanner, for creating this nightmare.* Finding the way out was up to her.

"They blame you for Tanner's death, Zoe, even without knowing that I'm Sam's father. Even if you're willing to subject yourself to that poisonous atmosphere, doesn't Sam deserve better?"

Of course he did. But to go to the Branchs', where she couldn't be sure of the reception, either… "They won't be unkind to Sam, not yet, at least. And I'm used to it."

"Zoe, my mother and brothers and sister are good people. They're Sam's family. They'll love him. Not one of them would deal him a moment's hurt."

You could, she thought as she stared at him. *And I'd have to pick up the pieces.*

An earnest man stared right back. He'd been thrown into this situation abruptly and was doing his best. "We should tell him now."

"No! Not yet. He's not ready."

One eyebrow rose. "He's not…or you're not?"

She wanted to curl up in a quiet room and not face any of this.

Will extended a hand slowly and clasped hers again. "Give me a chance, okay? I can't promise I won't make mistakes, but I swear that I'll do my best for Sam. He's a great kid, and I care about him already."

She felt the warmth of his big hand, the comfort of human touch, and it was all she could do to resist the urge to lean, just for a minute. She wanted to believe him, but... "I'm sorry. I can't. It's probably better, anyway, not to spring this on your mother at the last minute."

The strain in his face eased as his mouth curved. "Are you kidding? My mother lives for family."

"She can't know."

"She already does. I told you I wouldn't keep this from them." He smiled. "She's over the moon. She liked you, Zoe, surely you remember that. And she's dying to see Sam. If I hadn't promised to invite you, she'd be on your doorstep already."

"They can't tell Sam. And I'm not ready. I'll bring him to see her...soon. But not yet. And only with your family's promise not to reveal anything to him until I say so."

"They'll do whatever I ask." His jaw clenched. "But you and I are telling him soon. Very soon." He softened his voice again. "Don't be afraid, honey. It's going to be fine."

She eased from his grip, not one bit certain he was right. "Sam's bus is due any minute."

"Great. I'll go with you. Where do you meet him?"

Sam would be thrilled, but within her was a cold ball of foreboding she couldn't seem to shake. She didn't want him starting to rely on Will. Will was on vacation right now, but that would change.

But her child's father was looking at her with her child's eyes. With the eyes of the boy she'd once loved desperately.

"Zoe, please. Don't make this so hard," he said gently.

Nothing about this will ever be easy. She glanced away, fighting her weariness and lack of hope, and nodded. "This way." She began walking.

"WILL!" SAM LEAPED OFF the bus too quickly and stumbled. Tanner would have rolled his eyes or snorted at Sam's lack of coordination.

Will only looked delighted to see Sam. "Hey, dude, what's up? Glad school is going to be out for the holidays soon?"

He likes school, she started to say, but Sam answered first. "Yeah! I mean, yes, sir."

One eyebrow arched. "Nice manners, son."

Sam flushed. "Thanks."

Zoe wondered if Sam heard the emphasis on the word *son.* "How was your day, honey?"

He looked over at Will. "It was all right." Normally, he was full of comments and observations, details and little stories, but Will's presence was holding him back. Tanner had never liked what he called chatter.

"What's your favorite part of the school day?" Will asked.

She could see Sam's surprise. "Science. But I like to read, too."

At the same age, Will would have probably named a sport or said recess, she imagined.

"Ever dissected a frog?" he asked instead as they walked toward the apartment.

"Not yet," Sam said. "But I bet the girls will scream and stuff."

"Oh, yeah," Will said. "Bart and I would chase girls around the lab with frog and fish guts."

Sam laughed, a merry ringing sound she hadn't heard from him in quite some time. Will's answering smile was wide.

"Did you get in trouble?" Sam asked.

Will's gaze cut to hers first, then back. "Yep. And then

we got in trouble when we got home, too. My mom didn't go for things like that."

"My mom doesn't, either."

Zoe waited for Will to say something deprecating, but again he surprised her.

"Moms are probably the only reason guys survive. Left alone, we'd all be heathens. Ever read *Lord of the Flies?*"

Zoe was amazed that Will had. Reading had never been high on his list of favorite activities, to her knowledge. "That book is too old for you," she told Sam.

"Is it?" But Sam was looking to Will, not her, for the decision.

She definitely wasn't used to that. Nor did she like it one bit. "Yes—" she began.

"Yes and no," Will said at the same instant.

"I read stuff that's older than my age group. I'm a good reader."

Will looked to her for guidance. She folded her arms. He'd started this; let him tackle the tough subjects.

"I believe you," Will began. "I can tell you're really smart. I think what your mom is worried about is the subject matter. That book doesn't paint a pretty picture of human nature. I probably shouldn't have brought it up."

No, you shouldn't have, she thought.

"What's it about?" Sam asked.

"These boys who wind up on an island with no adults and have to create their own society."

"They fight, I bet," Sam said.

"They absolutely do."

"It might be interesting," Sam conceded as if humoring him, "but I like science stuff better."

"Then that's what you should read." Relief shone on Will's face that he'd dodged that bullet.

They'd reached the apartment door by then, and Zoe unlocked it.

"Can you stay?" Sam asked. "We could play video games." Hope shone in his eyes.

Despite that, Zoe wished with all her heart Will would say no. She hadn't slept well again, and being constantly on edge around him wasn't helping with her exhaustion level.

"Sure."

"Mom's not much on playing them."

"She can't help it. Not as many girls like them." Will's tone dripped with pity.

Zoe's ire rose. "This girl managed to beat you at Animal Crossing," she pointed out to Sam.

"Yeah, when I was, like, five."

Zoe did a double take at his cheeky response, the impish grin he hardly ever displayed.

The unusual flare of spirit seemed to tickle Will as much as it did her. His slashing grin was quick and devastating. "Well, you're an older guy now. Maybe you think you're ready for the big leagues." His tone was pure challenge.

Hot words sprang to her lips. He shouldn't be—

Sam's grin was quick. "Maybe your reflexes are old and slow."

She was stunned to see a Sam she'd never met. An only child, she'd been around boys too little. This was how Will and Bart behaved with each other, though, she recalled. Affection was not shown with hugs or tender words but more often by locking horns, verbally and physically.

Her little boy was being challenged—and challenging right back.

And glowing. She was amazed at how Will brought him out of his shell.

Will glanced at his watch. "You're on, buddy. I have to meet Bart in an hour or so. Plenty of time to destroy you." He rubbed his hands. "I haven't whipped a shrimp in too long."

Sam was full-on smiling now. "The bigger they are, the harder they fall."

"Oh, you are so going to regret that smart mouth of yours." Before Sam or Zoe could react, Will had grabbed Sam and slung him over his shoulder.

Zoe gasped, stepped forward.

But Sam only giggled, his blond hair bouncing with every step Will took down the hall.

Zoe watched them go and sank to the sofa in amazement.

And maybe a little hope.

She read a magazine. Tidied up a kitchen already too clean and stayed away—barely—from eavesdropping, then decided it wasn't eavesdropping to go ask if they wanted a snack. *Sure thing, Zoe, like Will is some neighbor kid here for a play date.* Heading to Sam's room, she dragged her feet more with every inch. What was she afraid of? That Sam was having a terrible time?

Or that he wasn't?

She wasn't used to sharing, she realized suddenly. Tanner had shown so little interest that most of Sam's life he'd been all hers. Zoe and Sam, a unit. Them against the world.

As she approached Sam's door, she caught a glimpse of the two of them—

And what she saw nearly broke her heart.

Each with his controller, the two of them were intent on the screen, their profiles so eerily reminiscent of one another she wondered how anyone in the world could have missed it.

Then her boy, her sweet little boy who was growing up much too fast, cast a quick glance up at Will, his eyes pure hero worship—and longing.

Zoe pressed one fist against her heart to still the dread that struck like an arrow. Will could do so much damage. Probably would, once the season began. He'd left her without a backward glance, hadn't he? Been perfectly clear that racing was still his life? She wanted to snatch Sam up and run, far and fast, to protect her baby's heart.

But then Sam turned his attention back to the screen and Will's gaze sought his child's face. He didn't look confused right now.

He looked proud. Amazed.

She must have made a noise because Will looked up and spotted her.

Give me a chance, his expression seemed to say. Just then Sam looked at Will to see why he'd paused, and his anxious expression made her heart hurt.

When Will tore his eyes from her and grinned at Sam, Sam visibly relaxed. Will nudged Sam with his shoulder, and Sam nudged right back—then giggled.

She wondered if Will had the faintest clue the power he wielded.

Her child was starving for a man in his life. For a dad. She had no right to deny him what he wanted so badly, but she was terrified of the harm Will could inflict.

That he would was almost certain, intentional or not. Will wasn't the staying kind. Zoe turned away quickly, barely able to breathe for the fear crowding her chest.

Before she gave in to it and sent Will packing.

And broke her son's heart herself.

SHE HEARD the whoops from Sam, then his footsteps as he pounded down the hall. "Mom, can I go with Will to meet his twin brother? That's Bart Branch, you know. He's a driver, too, the No. 475 car. He's pretty good, but I don't think he's as good as Will."

Will, coming up from behind him, sighed dramatically. "I tell him and tell him the same thing, but he just doesn't listen."

"I guess he's not the smart twin," Sam said, grinning.

"No question about it." They slapped high fives, Sam leaping to match Will's much-bigger palm.

"So can I, Mom? Please?"

"May I," she corrected.

"Moms can't help it," Will said.

"Yeah." The two exchanged grins and rolled their eyes.

In that instant, Zoe felt a jolt of resentment so strong it took her breath. It didn't matter that Sam was at an age where all girls had cooties; she'd been exempt. Who was Will to come barging in here and play the cool guy, the fun guy, and put her on the outside looking in?

"Whoa, now, dude," Will said, to her surprise. "Moms are girls, yes, but I think mine's the greatest, and I don't know what I'd do without her. I bet you feel the same."

Sam, ever sensitive to the currents around him, glanced back and forth between them uneasily. Zoe sought for something to say, but the barbs of resentment clung.

Will looked at his watch. "I've gotta go. What do you say, Zoe? Can he come with me?"

How did she know what he'd tell Sam about their relationship? Would Bart spill the truth?

Will was examining her more closely than she'd like. "On second thought, why don't you join us. Bart would like to see you again."

"Yeah, Mom, come with us!" Sam was bouncing on his toes, he was so excited.

"I don't—" But she could see Sam begin to droop, expecting the letdown. The last week had been a rough one. Things had been hard on Sam for a long time, but he never complained.

"Please, Mom?"

Will's gaze hadn't wavered. "Your mom doesn't have to. She might like some time alone."

No. Yes. She didn't know what she wanted, except for life to slow down and let her breathe.

"Give us a minute, will you, buddy?"

Sam's joy was fading. "Are you all right, Mom?"

"I'm fine, honey. Let me talk to Will a minute." She found a smile for him.

His feet dragged as he left the room.

"What's the problem, Zoe?"

How did she explain? She was just so frightened for Sam. Afraid of so much else, really, for years now.

But she was on her own again, and she had to figure out how to be brave. "I'll go," she conceded. "Let me get my purse."

"You don't trust me with him, is that it? I'm trying, can't you see that? What else can I do?"

"Stop pushing me, Will. I'm trying, too, but I can't… I don't…"

His expression went from frustration to worry. "Honey, you have to get some rest. You're exhausted, aren't you?"

She was, but that couldn't matter.

"Let me take him with me so you can get some sleep. I promise I won't tell him he's my son and neither will Bart. We'll care for him like he was fine china. You look worn out. You can't keep ignoring your health. You won't be any good to Sam if you wind up in the hospital."

She rubbed her forehead. "I can't think. I don't know what to do." She was getting light-headed again.

Will stepped close, wrapped one arm around her shoulders. "Zoe, please let me help you."

Don't be kind to me, Will. She steeled herself against the urge to nestle into him, the magnetism he still wielded to such devastating effect without even trying. *I can't afford to get sidetracked. This can't be about me or how easily I could fall for you again. All that matters is Sam.*

With his free hand, Will pulled out his phone.

"What are you doing?"

"I'm calling Bart to cancel."

She stepped out of his arms before she yielded further. What she couldn't do was spend one more minute in his presence. "No. Go ahead. Take Sam with you, just—"

"I don't think so. I'm worried about you."

"I'll be fine. I'll lie down, I promise." Anything to make him leave. She was too weary to fight her feelings anymore.

"You can trust me with him, I swear it. I'll have him back in two hours, max. I'll write down my cell number for you." He did so, then started for Sam's room, then halted. "I don't like leaving you like this."

"I'm okay, just—" *Weary to my soul.*

Will studied her for a long moment. "We'll wait until you're in bed. Does Sam have a key so we can lock the door behind us?"

"Stop hovering, Will. I'll see you out."

He looked skeptical but did as she asked, gathering up one very delighted child and ushering him out the door.

"Have fun," she forced herself to call out to Sam.

Sam waved but was practically dancing as he left with Will.

Take care of my boy, she pleaded silently as she watched them go. *He's all I've got.*

CHAPTER SEVEN

HE'D CALLED HER on Saturday to see how things went with the Hitchenses, but had been forced to leave a message. He'd watched football with his brothers. Eaten too much birthday cake. Tried to make things normal, when the elephant at the table was the boy who should have been with them.

Zoe didn't call back.

He'd called her on Sunday, too.

Same result.

He wanted to see Sam again, damn it. They'd had a great time with Bart, who'd taken to Sam as though they'd known each other forever. They'd found an arcade next to the ice-cream shop and blasted each other in galactic warfare, then pitted themselves against each other in a NASCAR racing game.

The boy had great reflexes. And a whip-smart intelligence. He still stumbled over his feet now and again, but shoot, his feet were huge, just as Will could remember his own being at that age.

Following in Dad's footsteps.

Dad. Holy cow. It still shocked him that he was a father.

He shot to his feet. The time he had to focus solely on Sam was dwindling. He had to leave to for testing at Halesboro later in the week, and damned if he'd let Zoe keep ducking any longer. He'd given her all the space she was going to get.

Sam would be in school. He'd checked. Downloaded a copy of the school calendar, so Zoe could never again consider him clueless on that account.

If she wasn't home, he'd sit there until she was. For sure she'd be back by the time Sam got home, and Bart had agreed to come get Sam if needed, so Will could have it out with her without worrying the boy. Bart was still going on the rock-climbing trip they'd planned even though Will had canceled, but he'd offered to delay a day.

Will's mom would have gladly helped out, since she was itching to meet Sam, but because Zoe hadn't yet agreed to tell Sam about his new family, Will hadn't wanted Maeve's first meeting with Sam to be a lie. His mother had had enough grief in the past year, and he wanted to give her the joy of being introduced to Sam as exactly what she was: his grandmother.

A kickass one she would be, too. Sam had no idea what a treat was in store for him.

Thinking of the longing on his mother's face at the birthday dinner and her excitement over Christmas shopping turned Will's mood more sour when he contemplated Zoe. Will recalled all the terrific holidays they'd had as kids and how Maeve could make any day special, for that matter. Zoe was robbing not only Maeve, but Sam, as well, of time they would never get back.

But Will couldn't focus on all that he and his family had missed of Sam's life. He was trying to cut Zoe a break because this problem was initially Tanner's doing and because her life wasn't easy—but there were limits. This stalemate had to end.

He was in a mood when he swung into the parking lot and spotted Zoe's car. Hot little licks of temper ate at his resolve to be reasonable. He knocked at her door with two sharp raps.

Simmered while he waited. Pounded this time. "Open up, Zoe."

When she finally did, he opened his mouth to blast her—

Until he got a look at her face. "What happened?" He shoved the door open and grabbed her. "Who hit you?"

She turned from him, trying to escape. "Go away, Will."

"Uh-uh." He forced her to face him, but gentled his hold even as fury sank claws into him. That soft ivory skin, marked by a purple shadow. "Who did this?" He touched her bruised cheek softly, but she still winced. "Talk to me, Zoe. Are you hurt anywhere else?"

She shook her head and stared at their feet. "I don't want to talk about it."

"Well, that's just too bad. Have you called the cops? Is Sam here? Oh, God, is Sam hurt, too?" He glanced around. "I have to get you out of this lousy neighborhood."

Her head drew up sharply. One harsh bark of laughter escaped. "This happened in your upscale enclave, for your information."

"My—" Recognition dawned. "Tanner's family? They hit you?"

She averted her eyes. "His mom slapped me. His dad stopped her after that."

"You told them."

A small nod.

"Oh, Zoe." He drew her in. "You should have let me go with you." His mouth firmed. "I'll take care of this, don't you worry. Louise Hitchens will regret losing control, I promise you that."

"Just let it go, please, Will."

Absolutely not, he thought. But he felt her tremble and didn't say anything else. The Hitchens family had a lot to answer for, beginning with how they'd treated Tanner, but he wouldn't add to Zoe's distress right now.

"Do you want to talk about it?" he asked.

Zoe shook her head.

"Sam's okay? Did he see it?"

Another shake. "He's fine. He was watching television in another room. I didn't intend to tell them yet, but Louise started in on how I'd ruined Tanner's life and how she would take Sam from me if it was the last thing she did, and—" She exhaled in a gust. "Anyway, I told Sam I walked into a door."

Sam was a bright kid. "He buy it?"

"I hope so."

Will tightened his arms around her. "Damn it, Zoe, why didn't you call me? I could have helped. You don't have to do everything alone."

Her voice was muffled, but he could make out the words, anyway.

I always have.

All his earlier anger at her evaporated. When she tried to draw back, instead he held on. *You're not alone now,* he wanted to say. *I'm here for you.*

But there were too many details unsettled between them yet. Too many complications. So he settled for pressing a kiss to her hair, then letting her go.

When his body was begging him to do so much more. She felt good, really good, against him.

She drew back, and her pupils were huge and dark with a mirrored temptation. It was all he could do not to grab her again. Instead he blurted out the first thing that came to mind. "I have to leave on Sunday for North Carolina."

Icy stillness moved over her. "I thought racing was done until after the holidays."

"It is the off-season, but my team has a testing session. Next year is huge for us, and we need more data. I have a sponsor that's still a little shaky, and I have to prove that their investment is worth it. I need to win."

"I see." She turned away. "Were you going to tell Sam?"

"Of course." Sudden inspiration struck. "I want him to come. Both of you," he amended.

"He's still in school."

"I know that. I have a school calendar now," he said defensively. "But it's only two days, and he's a good student, you said. I talked to Kylie Palmer, my PR rep. She has a son, Ryan, who's ten. She said schools can give makeup work. Sam could do ahead or take it with him. Kylie might drop in, too, and Sam would have a chance to meet Ryan, have someone his age to play with. He'd like him, I bet. Ryan's a good kid."

"It's out of the question."

"Why? Because it's me asking?" Resentment began to stir. "You want me to pay attention to him. This is a way to make him part of my life. And you know he'd enjoy it—admit it."

"It's disruptive. Anyway, I have job interviews. I don't have any money, remember? And now Sam won't, either. The Hitchenses promised they'd fight the will every step of the way."

"Then we'll get a better lawyer," Will said.

"You heard Howard," she said. "Tanner very carefully kept nearly everything separate."

"That bastard," Will exploded. Then he settled. "Even so, I'll get you a lawyer. Anyway, I'll take care of you. I told you that."

"I'm not your responsibility, Will."

"Sam is," he pointed out. "And you could be."

Her expression froze. "I don't want to be."

He absorbed the zing. Tried not to let it get to him. "Be that as it may, our lives are joined now, Zoe. We'll never be completely separate again. If nothing else, I will pay support for Sam, and I don't want him being a latchkey kid. I make good money, and I will take care of both of you. You don't have to get a job."

"What if I want to?" Her chin took on a stubborn tilt.

Easy, buddy. In this day and age, you didn't tell a woman she couldn't pursue a career.

Even if you believed her child was better off with her at home. "Do you?" He was sincerely curious. "What is it that you want to do, Zoe?"

Her shoulders sank. "I don't know." She glared at him. "Except to make sure my child is safe and healthy and happy."

Her doubts about his ability to help with that were obvious, and Will's temper stirred again.

She's just nervous, honey. Her life has been turned upside down. His mother's words echoed in his head and made him look more closely at Zoe.

And chill out. *Be honest.* "That's what I want, too. Sam's a great kid. You've done an amazing job with him."

Her eyes went wide.

"I mean it," he continued. "I don't want to get in your way, and I'm not trying to hem you in. It's just that, well, I was lucky enough to have my mom around all the time when I was growing up, and even if I was a stupid kid who took it for granted that she'd always be there, I see now what that meant. She was always there for us, and not just to make us clean our rooms or take a bath or get our homework done." Zoe's eyes had softened, so he went on. "She took us to Little League and watched every game, every practice. She decorated the house like crazy for each holiday. She loves to cook, and there was always something great to eat when we got home from school." He shrugged. "My dad wanted her to be a social butterfly, and he gave her a lot of grief that she resisted, but she quietly did things her own way and focused on what was most important to her—which, thank God, was us. If any of us is worth a damn as a human being, it's because of her."

He took Zoe's hand. "When my father pulled his vanishing act earlier this year, she wasn't in much better shape than you are because she'd never worked outside the home. I understand that it's a risk for you, Zoe. And I'm promising you that I'll take steps right now to set up some security for you, if you decide that being with Sam is what's most important to you."

"Will, I'm not asking—" She tugged at her hand.

He didn't let go. "I know you're not. I'm just saying that Sam's had a lot of upheaval in his life, and he's going to have more when he finds out about me. Maybe he'll be happy and maybe he won't, but whatever his reaction, I'm guessing he'll need you more than ever. I'd like to do what I can to help on that score. Mothers can make up for a lot of bad fathering, and I can tell you already have. Maybe I won't be any good as a dad, no matter how hard I try. But regardless, if I can make it possible for you to not be so worried about money so that you can take time to figure out what you want to do, I think that's only good for Sam, don't you?"

She bit at her lips, and her eyes got really shiny. She nodded. "But—"

"No buts, Zoe. Whatever was between us in the past, what matters to both of us is Sam." When one tear spilled over, he reeled her in and clasped her chin in one hand. "Truce? Can we stop fighting each other for Sam's sake? Could we start over, honey?"

"Will, I...I'm—"

Afraid. She might as well say it aloud. He knew he'd earned that lack of faith years before. Had done little so far to show her that he could be different.

You'll be a wonderful father.

Oh, Mom, I don't know. He was ready to let go, to give up.

But Zoe touched his cheek just then. "I'm being a coward. You're right, and I'd like to start over." Her eyes were gray velvet, sweet and sad and serious.

And I'd like to kiss you, Will thought. *Not as my child's mother, but simply as...you.* With an ache in his heart for his past mistakes with her, he bent his head closer. When he heard Zoe's intake of breath, he tensed, wondering if she would flee.

Then he surprised himself by not diving in as he once would have but only brushing his lips softly over hers, a symbol of a promise, a vow.

When Zoe lingered instead of running, clutched at his sides instead of shoving him away, Will found inside himself an unexpected tenderness that kept his growing desire in check. He wrapped his arms around her and tried not to think about the body so close against his own and all the ways he'd like to be even closer.

Because, he was discovering, Zoe herself—her heart, her peace of mind—was even more important to him.

After a precious few seconds, she eased away. "I guess we could start by trying one trip. If you really want us with you at Halesboro." She lifted one shoulder. "You're right. He's an excellent student. A couple of days won't kill him."

The tightness in Will's chest eased. "Thank you." But he couldn't let it rest there, not when he'd been thinking about his mother. "What about my family? What about telling Sam who I really am?"

She closed her eyes, then opened them. "Could we please wait until we get back? Take this one step at a time?"

Patience. He'd need a boatload of it, he could see.

But he'd said he cared about her as well as Sam, so it was time to put up or shut up. "All right. After we get back."

"I'm sorry, Will. It's nothing against your family. I like your mom a lot. I'm just trying…" She faltered. "I'm doing my best, I swear it."

The tension was back, and he didn't want that. "It's okay, Zoe. I get it. I have a lot to prove to you." He looked away to keep from revealing his disappointment.

You're too blasted impatient, Will, Taney had said, over

and over. *You'll be a better driver when you learn that some things just can't be forced.*

Taney would probably get a kick out of knowing that life was ramming that lesson down Will's throat.

CHAPTER EIGHT

THE TRACK AT HALESBORO was not a pretty sight, Zoe thought as they drove up. She and Sam had had to fly separately from Will, and for a second she wondered if Mike, the team member who'd been sent to pick them up in Charlotte, had taken the wrong route.

"Wow, this place is a dump," Sam said.

Zoe glared at him.

"Sorry," Sam responded.

Mike looked over his shoulder. "This track is a legend, son. Doesn't look like much now, but it's got a rich history."

"It was on the circuit from the 1950s until eight years ago, Mom," Sam explained.

Mike grinned. "You know your NASCAR, huh? Will said you were smart as a whip."

Sam's eyes widened. "He did?"

Zoe tensed, wondering what else Will might have said.

"And begging your pardon, miss, but he was right about you, too. Said you were a looker. Real classy, too. Said you and he were old friends but he'd just met your boy." He winked at Sam. "He's hoping you won't be bored."

"Oh, no, sir!" Sam was practically jittering on the seat.

"I'll check to see where he is, then take you to him." Mike emerged from the car and strode to a knot of men near the grandstands.

"This is so cool, Mom. Do you know how many legendary drivers raced here?"

She had to smile. She stroked his hair. "No, but I bet you can tell me." Her trepidation over the trip had increased tenfold, but now that she saw Sam's excitement, she couldn't regret coming. Typical of Sam, he'd finished all his homework on the plane. Now he was ready for nothing but racing.

Mike returned. "He's on the track right now. I can take your bags over to the bus once I show you where to watch—unless you'd rather go there instead."

"Bus?" she asked.

He nodded. "Will had me bring his motor home here, so you'd have a comfortable place to stay."

She frowned. "I thought we'd be in a motel."

"Not a good idea. Once the track lost its NASCAR Sprint Cup race date, combined with the fact that its biggest factory shut down, this town went downhill fast. This is better, believe me. The motor home is like a hotel on wheels, only more comfortable." He smiled. "And I'm a darn good cook."

But…where would Will be staying? Her insides gave a little shiver, but she quickly tamped down her reaction. Just because he'd held her close, kissed her once…been ready to tackle Tanner's parents on her behalf….

No. She was never getting sidetracked by Will Branch again. No matter how wonderful it had felt to be in his arms. How great his muscled body had felt against her.

Then she realized that both Mike and Sam were looking at her expectantly. She wanted to retreat, to avoid Will as long as possible—

But Sam's eyes were shining.

"I guess we'd like to watch Will first, right?" she asked Sam.

Sam bounced once on the seat. "Yeah!" In an instant, he was climbing from the car.

Zoe had no choice but to follow.

WILL BARRELED into the garage area, frustrated as hell. The car had been loose all through the corners earlier, but now it was tight in the middle and loose off, plus the tires were chattering like crazy on this lousy track surface. He was hot and tired, and testing was not his favorite activity.

He and his crew chief, Seth Gallant, were barely speaking. Seth had finally told him over the radio that if he couldn't quit bitching to just shut up.

"Seth, it's too blasted tight in the middle." Will yanked off his helmet, raked fingers through his sweaty hair and got ready to climb from the car and have it out.

"Will" said a delighted young voice. "That was awesome!"

His ill humor evaporated under the light of Sam's million-watt smile. "Hey, buddy. You made it."

Sam took a step toward him, then halted uncertainly. His eyes kept darting toward the inside of the car.

Will found that he could grin, after all. "Want to see?"

Sam's head whipped around. "I can look?"

"You can do better than that." He swiveled and climbed over the door, then picked Sam up and slid him into the driver's seat.

Sam's eyes were big as saucers. Dinner plates. He started to touch, then froze.

Damn you, Tanner, for making this child doubt himself.

"I bet you know already what that is," Will said gently.

"Is it the tachometer?"

"Sure is."

"And this is the fuel pressure gauge."

"You got it." He really was a bright boy. Pride burgeoned inside him.

"Will, what are you doing outside the—" Seth rounded the open hood and halted.

"I'm showing—" *My boy,* Will almost said. His promise to Zoe stuck in his craw. "—Sam here around the inside.

Sam—" he prodded the boy, who was greedily eating up every detail as if he'd be yanked out any second "—this is my crew chief, Seth Gallant. Seth, this is Sam…Hitchens." He didn't like using that last name one bit.

"Pleased to meet you, sir," Sam said. "You used to be Kent Grosso's car chief, right?"

Seth arched one brow, glanced at Will, impressed. "That's right. Four years."

"And you raced yourself, on dirt tracks."

Seth's brow rose higher. "In high school, yes." Then his attention was distracted by something behind them.

Will glanced back.

And saw her.

Zoe stood at the entrance, poised like a doe ready to run. She was dressed simply in pale blue slacks and a matching sweater, a single strand of pearls around her slender white throat, her white-blond hair gently brushing her shoulders. She was a vision, slender and delicate, for all that she was fairly tall for a woman.

He realized that he was as tongue-tied as the rest of them and rose from his crouch. "You made it." He was only marginally aware of all the curious looks around him. He'd had his share of female guests on race weekends, but he'd never brought a woman to testing before. Certainly not one with a child. *We can't keep this a secret forever, Zoe.* And he was perversely glad, though he hadn't invited them here to force her hand.

He bent to Sam. "Don't touch anything, or Seth will kill us both."

Very seriously, Sam nodded.

Will walked to where Zoe stood, then flicked a glance at Mike. "All settled in?"

"I'm taking their bags over to the motor home now," Mike answered. "Thought I'd put together a snack, in case anyone gets hungry." A motor home driver was often the driver's cook, as well, and Will had been lucky with Mike. He could do a lot more than barbecue. He said cooking relaxed him, and Will was the beneficiary.

"Thanks, Mike," Will answered, but he only had eyes for Zoe. He extended a hand. "Want to come see what Sam's doing?"

She glanced around, obviously out of her element, a gentle, feminine presence in a world of grease and metal and rubber. "I don't want to be in the way. Maybe I should just—"

"No one will bite—well, except Seth, but he mostly barks, and he does that to all of us." Will caught the grins of the team. Seth was a great crew chief, but he was intense and driven. He was the first to praise a good performance, but he didn't mind peeling a strip off your hide, either.

"I heard that," Seth said.

Will took her hand and drew her over the garage threshold. "Zoe Hitchens, this is Seth Gallant." He went around the space, introducing the two engineers, his car chief and the mechanics present. "Zoe is Sam's mother." The explanation seemed lame in comparison to her impact on his life, past and present. More than ever, he was eager to dispense with the lies.

Zoe's smile was hesitant. "Hello," she said to the group in general. "I'll just get Sam and move out of the way. I know you're all busy, and I—"

"We can always make time for another gearhead, right, guys?" Will glanced around at the men assembled, who nodded. "It's how we all got our start, Zoe. Hanging out in garages. Besides—" he gestured at Sam "—the way this boy absorbs information, by the end of the day, he'll probably be teaching us a thing or two."

Sam ducked his head, his cheeks flaring.

But he had a huge grin on his face, and Zoe noticed. She quit resisting Will and instead favored him with a grateful glance.

Will looked down at her with a smile and managed to restrain himself from kissing her again, however much he was tempted.

But he didn't let go of her hand.

"So if it's too blasted tight in the middle, what do you do?" Sam asked.

Several team members, Seth included, chuckled.

Will returned his attention to his son, chagrined—and glad he hadn't said worse. He let go of Zoe and bent down next to Sam.

Trying his best not to be distracted by his son's beautiful mother.

THEY'D DO some night testing, too, Seth had decided suddenly, but with Halesboro's lousy lighting, Will was happy he'd be the only car on the track. Meanwhile, the team had a couple of hours off to grab a bite and chill while Seth figured out his setups.

Sam was chattering a mile a minute. "That's so cool, listening on the headsets to you and Seth. I always wondered what you said to each other during practice."

He had made a concerted effort to keep his language clean, and Seth had, too.

That would have to be his life from now on, Will realized, now that Sam was in it. Sure, millions could listen in on them either at the track or on the Internet or the radio during a race, but Will was accustomed to that. Practice, garage time and life in general was different.

Man, being a parent was a whole new world.

"Glad you enjoyed it. You didn't get bored out there?"

Sam's eyes flew wide. "No way!"

Which was more than Will could say for Zoe, who'd been very quiet all afternoon…and was almost visibly stiffening with every step they took now. He wanted to ask what was wrong with her—but not where Sam could hear. Anyway, they were overdue for a heart-to-heart on revealing the truth to Sam.

"Will Branch?" A man stepped from the shadow of the motor home.

Will put an arm around Zoe and pulled Sam behind him. "What do you want?"

Nearly Will's height, the man stayed where he was and pulled a badge from his coat pocket. "Detective Lucas Haines, NYPD. I have some questions to ask you."

Zoe gasped, and Sam moved closer to Will.

Hell. Great timing, Detective. "Give me a minute." Will led them to the steps of the motor home, and opened the door.

A very unhappy Mike stood inside. "Sorry, man. He wouldn't let me warn you."

"What's this about, Will?" Zoe asked. "Why is he here? What does he want with you?"

Will glanced at Sam's worried gaze, then met hers again. "I'm sure it's nothing." He tried to convey confidence to her with his eyes, then addressed Mike. "You take care of them while I'm gone. I won't be long." He turned away, but not before he saw the confusion and distrust on Zoe's face, how she clasped Sam's shoulders. The worry on Sam's features.

Will paused and dropped to a crouch. "It's really okay, buddy, I promise." But Sam didn't relax at all. The bubbling joy had vanished. For that alone, Will wanted to level the man outside.

But that was the hothead Will's way. He was a father now, and he had to put Sam first.

Even if visions of his own father in handcuffs leaped to his mind instantly.

Will rose. "I swear I've done nothing wrong," he told Zoe. He summoned a smile and ruffled Sam's hair. "Save me some supper, okay, champ?"

Sam's eyes were anxious, but he nodded. "I will."

Zoe nodded. "We'll be here." *And you will explain,* her expression seemed to say.

Will glanced at Mike and took comfort from knowing that Mike had his back and would watch over them. He stepped out of the motor home and approached the dark-haired man waiting for him. "Let's take it away from here," he said curtly and started walking.

When they were a good distance from everyone at the track, Will pivoted. "I don't appreciate you popping up like this."

"Got a job to do. You've been far away." The cop's manner was intense, but he did ease up a bit. "Sorry for worrying your family, though."

Will tensed. "They're just friends."

Haines shrugged. "Sorry. Boy bears a strong resemblance to you, so I thought—"

Time is up, Zoe. But he didn't explain. "This is about Alan Cargill, right?"

Haines didn't concur or deny. "You left the NASCAR Awards Banquet suddenly. Why?"

"I found out right before the dinner that my best friend had died and the funeral was to be the next day."

"Why not wait until after the dinner—or leave before?"

"You don't understand NASCAR, do you, Detective?"

"I understand pre-meditated murder."

"Pre-meditated?" Will's eyes popped. "I thought it was a mugging." He stepped back. "You can't possibly think—"

"I'm just collecting information, Mr. Branch. We're interviewing a lot of people, trying to see who might have wanted Mr. Cargill out of the picture. Might have something to hide. Tell me what you know about Brent Sanford."

"You mean the cheating scandal?" Sanford's career had ended in disgrace four years before when he'd been accused of tampering with Kent Grosso's car. Alan Cargill had pointed the finger at Brent. "He sure doesn't like Alan, but that doesn't make him a murderer. Was he even there? He stays away from the circuit altogether, from what I hear."

"Do you think he cheated?"

Will shrugged. "I don't know. Never thought about it a lot. I was just coming into NASCAR then, and I was focused on my own career."

"So you don't know Brent Sanford well?"

"Not really. No more than anyone else does."

"They've had several public arguments. The animosity between them is intense. Did you see him in New York?"

"No. As I said, he avoids anything related to NASCAR like the plague. Why are you asking me about him? I told you, I don't really know him." After the media circus his family had been through, Will would never willingly subject anyone else to that scrutiny.

"But you knew Cargill. Wanted to drive for him once, correct?"

Will frowned, trying to keep up with the switch in topic. "Yeah. I really wanted a NASCAR Sprint Cup ride with Cargill Motorsports."

"Kent Grosso stood in your way, didn't he?"

Will frowned. "What are you implying?"

"Not a thing," Haines said. "Just noting the facts. You were the one who'd benefit most from Grosso's poor performance in Talladega. He blows it, you're next in line for the ride."

Will's hands fisted. "You can't be saying I was the one who sabotaged his car. I would never do that. Anyone knows that."

"People didn't expect your father to embezzle millions and vanish, either."

"Are you saying like father, like son?" Will stepped forward. "You son of a bitch. I'm not like him. I'm *nothing* like him. I hate his guts."

"You want to back up, Mr. Branch. This is only a friendly interview, but that could change if you want to threaten me."

"*You're* threatening *me,*" Will said. "My family has been through hell, and none of us needs more scandal."

"If Alan Cargill suspected you of the sabotage, that would have been a scandal, too, right?"

Will's stomach dropped to his feet. "Are you seriously accusing me of foul play? I wasn't even there when Alan Cargill died. I was on my way to Texas."

"I'm not accusing anyone, Mr. Branch. Just gathering information, I told you. I need you to trace your steps that night from the time you left the table until you got on the plane. What flight did you take?"

"Taney sent me on his plane—Gideon Taney, my team owner." Will's head was reeling from the notion that he could be a suspect. His family…Zoe. Oh, God, Zoe. This could undo every inch of progress they'd made.

And then there was his sponsor, McKay Lundgren. "Look, I had nothing to do with Cargill's death. I had no part in the sabotage of Kent's car. I'll cooperate with you fully, but please—for my family's sake—could you keep my name out of it? My mother is just now recovering, my brother has the same pressures I do to keep his sponsor and Penny's and Sawyer's lives are only beginning to settle down."

Haines looked at him steadily for a long moment. At last he spoke. "You're not at the top of my list, Branch. Unfortunately, no one is yet. But I have to cover the bases, you understand. A man is dead, and he deserves justice." He paused. "Give me a few more details, and I'll pursue them. If they check out, I'll do what I can to clear you soon."

Will thought about all the man-hours that had gone into tracking his father down, into making the case against him. "I know you're only doing your job. I'm innocent, and you'll see that, but—damn. I just want to drive my race car. Get back to a normal life," he said wearily.

"I don't think there's much about a driver's life that's normal, Mr. Branch, but I hear you. For the record, I didn't expect you to have company. I'm sorry if I upset your—the boy."

"It's okay." Though it wasn't. But Will wanted to be finished with this. To get back and see how much damage this had done to the truce with Zoe, to be sure Sam was all right.

"All right. Got your paper and pen handy?"

"Ready when you are," Haines replied.

CHAPTER NINE

From the doorway of Will's bedroom in the motor home, Zoe watched Will saying good-night to Sam. An unspoken truce had gotten them through a delicious meal of chicken fajitas, while Mike had provided a blessed distraction by telling Sam story after story about life on the racing circuit—thereby preventing any discussion of the homicide detective's visit beyond Will's perfunctory assurance that everything was fine.

Sam might buy it; Zoe did not. The strain in Will was obvious to her, but he'd done a good job of hiding it from Sam.

They would, however, be discussing the matter in detail once Sam was down. The way his eyes were drooping after the day's excitement, he'd be fast asleep in seconds. Would likely never stir when she joined him in the big bed later.

Another issue to deal with, as well: Will's intent to sleep here, too, albeit on the sofa. She was not the slightest bit comfortable having him that close.

Though, to be honest, she had to admit—to herself, at least—that the reason had nothing to do with fear of Will. It did, however, have everything to do with her increasing awareness of him as a man. A very attractive, very sexy, very—oh, it was so easy, too easy, to remember exactly how Sam had come to exist, and Will's magnetism had only increased with age. The boy who'd been her first lover was all grown up now, deliciously so.

She remembered a lot about him, more every day of all

that she'd managed to suppress for ten years: that he could be kind, could be funny, had this irrepressible energy that drew you. Only now there was a spice to him, a mystery, shaded with a dark pencil of sorrow. Of a vulnerability she'd never expected to find in him.

There was also, of course, that body her fingers itched to touch. Her own body roused to the siren call of the only man who'd ever shown her heights of glory she'd given up on reaching since.

And that was when he'd been much less experienced himself. Zoe repressed a delicious shiver at the very notion of what he might be like now.

Just then, Will rose and snapped her back to the present.

Where she was someone's mother, not a lover. No wide-eyed girl. She stood aside carefully to let Will pass, then gave Sam one last kiss on his forehead. "'Night, sweet-heart. Sweet dreams."

"'Night, Mom," he slurred, eyes too heavy to open.

She stroked his hair and watched him for a minute. Contemplated crawling into the bed now and having nothing more to do with Will tonight.

But…no. She had questions, and Will would have to answer them, like it or not. She rounded the bed, deliberately shutting out thoughts of the women who'd shared it with Will, this masculine haven of dark brown wood, honey-gold carpet and drapes, touches of the burnt orange of his beloved Texas alma mater added here and there.

She closed the door carefully, took a deep breath, then proceeded down the short hallway and into the living area, already composing her first question.

"We have to tell him, Zoe."

She blinked. "What?" She struggled to catch up to this very different tangent.

"Detective Haines guessed, just from looking at Sam. Called him my boy."

She frowned. "What did you say?"

He rolled his eyes. "I stuck to your script, of course, but he wasn't fooled, and from the scrutiny others are giving him, they aren't, either. If we don't tell him, someone else is going to, that simple."

She didn't like being on the defensive, so she turned the tables. "Tell me what's going on with the detective," she snapped.

He glared at her. "Don't change the subject."

"I'm not saying a word to Sam until I know what's going on. Why you're being questioned."

A muscle jumped in his jaw. "It's nothing."

"Sam's not here now. That won't fly. Something's wrong, and you owe me an explanation."

He rose from the sofa and began to pace. He stopped, facing away from her and raked both hands through his hair. At last, he exhaled sharply and turned, his face a study in exhaustion. "I do think it's going to be okay, honestly. I just wish—" He shook his head. "I've done nothing wrong, Zoe. Not that you should believe that, given who my father is."

In that moment, she figured out the source of the shadows. Pain vied with resentment and a measure of confusion. "You had nothing to do with your father's crimes." She could give him that much.

"I'm not so sure. I keep wondering if we played a part— the racing," he explained. "He sponsored both our teams, Bart's and mine, and racing's a very expensive proposition. He spent a lot on us, said he was so proud." His glance was anguished. "Did my family, my mother, especially, have to go through all this because he couldn't tell us he couldn't afford it?"

Guilt. That was part of the shadows, too. Zoe felt her distrust ebbing. "You didn't push him into it, Will. He pushed you. No one knows better than me how intense he was about your racing."

"I should tell you again how sorry I am."

She gauged him to be sincere. Patted the sofa beside her. "Come here." After a brief hesitation, he complied. Sagged into the cushions, as dispirited as she'd ever seen him.

"You're nothing like your father, if that's what's worrying you."

"How can I know that?" He tensed, sat forward. "How do I make sure I never do that to Sam? How can I even begin to think I can be the father he deserves, given the example my own set?"

Her heart melted. She laid one hand on his thigh. Thought about all sorts of arguments, then settled on the one she hoped would be most effective. "Because you know what it's like to be a trophy son." His quick glance, skeptical but full of wistfulness, made her continue. "Don't forget that your mother raised you much more than Hilton ever did, and she's as warm and giving a parent as I've ever met."

He lifted his gaze to hers. "You're that way, too, you know. Don't sell yourself short. Sam's really lucky to have you."

Her chest grew tight. "Thank you."

"I mean it. You're fantastic with him. He's amazing, and you're the reason why."

The warmth in his eyes traveled straight to her heart. "He was always wonderful. I can't take credit."

"You should." Will lifted a hand, caressed her cheek. "You're pretty amazing yourself."

Zoe's throat clogged, and tears prickled. "Thank you," she said huskily.

"No, the gratitude is mine. Thank you for keeping my boy safe." He moved in. "Thank you for giving me a chance to know him."

Zoe laid her hand over his, closed her eyes. Couldn't speak as Will's lips brushed hers once, twice...then slanted to seek entrance.

Longing suffused her, a tender mingling of gratitude and growing desire. Caution rose, but she let it go, just for now. Just for this moment.

Will became her only reality, his touch, his taste, his strong arms. "Zoe…" His mouth cruised her jaw, then down her throat. Zoe let her head fall to one side, granted him access.

The sweet hunger she'd repressed for ten years began to rise inside her, and Zoe reeled from the onslaught. She moaned from deep in her throat, her fingers clutching at the powerful muscles of his arms as she struggled not to drown in the spell he was weaving.

Smoothly, he lifted her to his lap. Began working the buttons of her blouse. Zoe kept her eyes closed, arched over one strong arm.

Bliss, oh, this was such bliss, so welcome, so tantalizing, this rapture—

A cell phone startled them. Had Will cursing under his breath.

She sat bolt upright. Shoved away from his embrace. What on earth was she thinking?

He grabbed her wrist, kept her close. "I'm sorry. Haines said he'd call if he had questions. I have to take this, damn it."

Zoe yanked herself free. Buttoned her blouse with shaking fingers. Fastened it all the way to the top this time.

After a brief, murmured conversation, Will snapped the phone shut and approached her. "Zoe, I—"

She held up a palm. "Don't. That shouldn't have happened. I need to—" She looked around frantically. "I have to go." She started for the door. Outside. Anywhere. Just away from him.

He caught her arm, tried to turn her around.

She slapped at his hand. "Don't touch me."

He held out both palms. "All right. Just…slow down, Zoe.

Don't—" He paused, his gaze intent. "Please don't leave. I will, if you insist on being alone. You can't be wandering around out there in the dark. This track has no security to speak of."

She paused with her hand on the doorknob. "I can't breathe. I need some air."

He gave a strained laugh. "You and me both." He considered. "How about we both go outside?"

If Sam weren't here, she'd be gone so fast Will's head would spin—but Sam *was* here. She couldn't leave him. "All right." Stiffly, she descended the steps. Took in several deep breaths.

"I'm not going to apologize for wanting you."

"It doesn't mean anything." She lifted a shoulder, her arms crossed over her chest. "What happened in there."

His chuckle was more genuine this time. "Good luck on believing that." In two strides, he was in front of her. Laid a scorching kiss on her.

Zoe's head spun again. She couldn't even summon the strength to push him away, not when she still wanted to climb all over him.

To her surprise, Will let go instead. In the light from the motor home, she took comfort from seeing that his triumph was marked by confusion, as well. "Don't kid yourself. It means something. We're not finished with each other, not by a long shot." Then he stepped back. "But I owe you some answers." His eyes narrowed. "And we still have to discuss telling Sam."

"No. Absolutely not." Her reaction was knee-jerk, but she wouldn't back down.

She could see hot words dancing on his lips. To his credit, he stifled them. Studied her before replying. Exhaled in a gust. "That's not realistic, honey."

"Don't call me honey."

The old Will would have lost his temper, but somewhere

he found more control. Actually chuckled. "You didn't used to be so unreasonable."

Her own shot into the red zone. "Protecting my child isn't unreasonable, you, you—"

His smile was infuriating. Then he sobered. "He's my child, too, Zoe. And he will get hurt if we don't tell him. Too many people can see the resemblance. Someone will blurt it out. Wouldn't you rather control the time and place?"

"If we stay away from racing, from you, he'll be fine."

She'd pushed him too far, she could tell. His jaw tightened. "You're not getting rid of me. I'm in for the duration. I don't want to fight you on this, sweetheart." Very white teeth flashed without amusement. "As a matter of fact, fighting you is way down on the list of what I'd like to do with you." The husky timbre of his voice made her shiver with memory of what they'd been doing only moments before. "But I will if you force me."

Just as she was about to slap back at him, his demeanor eased. "Please, Zoe, for Sam's sake, let's get along."

Oh, he was too good. "Low blow. You know I'll do anything for him."

Another smile, this one genuine, if tainted a little by triumph. "Finding weak spots in the competition is my job— but let's don't make this about competition." He moved closer, his voice silky. "Cooperation is so much more fun."

Zoe took a step back, but the motor home stopped her. "Keep your distance."

"I don't think so." Smooth, predatory as a panther, Will approached until only a breath of air separated their skin. "Come back inside with me." He captured her mouth in a bone-melting kiss.

She didn't manage to stifle a small moan. Will's arms slid around her, and she found him hard to resist.

But she had to. She broke free and sidestepped him. "Talk, Will. Keep your hands to yourself. Tell me what's going on."

He batted his head against the side of the motor home, though not hard.

Zoe couldn't help giggling. "Come on, it's not that bad."

He leveled her with a sideways glance that was both wicked and cheerful. Full of promise. "You're killing me, babe."

"You're tough," she teased, amazing herself. "You can take it."

A growl of pure male frustration emerged. "We'll make a trade. Talk now, action later." His eyebrows waggled. "Deal?"

She couldn't believe he was making her smile, not when they had so much that was serious to tackle. "You have always been incorrigible. I thought you'd grow out of it."

"That's not what I'm growing out of right this second."

She swatted his arm, then assumed a more sober stance, even though a part of her was astonished at how he could make her feel hopeful. Lighter. "Tell me about the detective."

Will leaned back against the metal, sighed. "You are a hard woman." His gaze was fond, though. "Do you know who Alan Cargill is?"

She shook her head.

"Sam and I have a lot of work ahead of us, I can tell." But he grinned as he began to explain.

When he got to the part where Haines had said he was a suspect, Zoe was incensed. "How can he possibly think you could do either? You'd never sabotage anyone. You're far too honorable for that—too competitive, too. You want to win, but not that way. And you'd certainly never kill a man. That detective is a fool if he thinks—"

Will's delighted laughter stopped her as he picked her up and whirled her. Set her down and kissed her before she could object. "Shoot, why did I bother talking to the man? I should have sent you in my place."

"You're joking, I know, but it's true. Do I need to call him and explain?"

"I don't think so. I gave him all the details he wanted, and he was calling just now for a couple of clarifications, but he said not to worry over it, assuming everything I told him checks out."

"It will."

He drew her close, pressed a tender kiss to her forehead. "Thank you for believing in me."

She looked up at him, relishing the feel of being in his arms. He made her feel protected, cherished. It was too inviting, too comfortable.

She stepped away. "About Sam."

He observed her cautiously. "Yes?"

"I just don't want him hurt."

"Knowing I'm his father will hurt him?" He visibly began closing in on himself. "I guess… I mean, with what my father has done, I can see why you wouldn't—"

She touched his arm. "You are not responsible for your father, Will. And it's not that. It's just…we have to be careful about what expectations we create in Sam. He'll be thrilled to find out you're his dad. But you don't know yet how much you want to be a part of his life—"

"I do," he interrupted. "I want to be his dad. I want us to be a family."

"That's…that's…" She faltered. "I'm happy for Sam, but there are so many complications, given your schedule. He can't just come be with you at the track, not when there's school, and I don't know what my job situation will be—"

"I meant all of us, Zoe. Sam, you and me."

"No." She shook her head violently. "That's not part of the deal. I don't…I can't…"

His face darkened. "Why not? We were good together once, weren't we?"

Until you walked away, yes. I thought we were much more than good. I thought we were perfect. She couldn't go through that again. Couldn't let it happen to Sam, either. She didn't trust him not to choose racing over her. "It's out of the question. If you want to talk about visitation schedules, that's one thing, and only sensible, figuring out how they would work before we tell Sam. But don't you dare start talking to him about being a family. That's not going to happen."

"I screwed up, all right? I should have stood up for you, for us. How long are you going to hold that against me?"

"I'm a realist. Racing is your life, and I'm not kidding myself otherwise. I won't let you fool Sam, either." When he cursed violently, she held up a hand. "I don't want to fight with you, Will. As you pointed out, that's not good for Sam, and Sam has to be the only consideration." She waited for his fury to subside.

It did. A colder version of the man who'd held her, tantalized her, cherished her only moments before stood in front of her now. "So what's your plan? I'm sure you have one, right, Queen of Control?"

She swallowed to dislodge the lump of his contempt. Her shoulders sagged in defeat. "Do you see why this can't work? We'll only confuse and worry Sam if we can't get along."

"We were getting along really well a few minutes ago," he reminded her.

She couldn't let herself remember that, though every second was seared on her brain. "We're supposed to be adults, Will, not horny kids."

The look he shot her could have scorched a stone. "What I feel for you is definitely adult, babe."

"This isn't about sex."

"And more's the pity. Sex is simple."

That generated a wry smile from her. "Not with you, it's not."

Amazingly, the atmosphere lightened. "Don't kid yourself that we won't be getting back to it, Zoe. There's too much heat between us." He glanced away. "But you're right. Sam is the most important thing. You're mistaken on one count, though. You don't trust me, and I understand that. But mark my words—" he pointed a finger at her "—I will prove you wrong. I'm going to make you trust me, and I will show you that I can be a good dad to Sam. And then—" The cocky driver was back. "Then I'm coming after you, sweetheart. Both gun barrels blazing."

Something in her quivered deliciously at the notion. She wasn't telling him, though. The stakes were far too high. "What's your schedule tomorrow?"

"Laps and laps, until I go blind. Or die of boredom."

She grinned at his resignation. "Sam's an early riser." Her smile widened. "You'll learn to regret that."

"Getting up early won't kill me."

She decided to leave him to his illusions. He'd missed the worst part, anyway, the sleep-deprived nights of infancy, the toddler who woke at the crack of dawn.

And because she was newly reminded of all he'd missed, she'd try harder to bring him into their lives. "If we tell him before you go out to drive, he'll have the whole day to brag. Are you really ready for that?"

"Absolutely." Not a scrap of hesitation.

"What about the PR angle? That's big news."

He stilled. Swore. "That's Kylie's problem. I'll call her in a few minutes, give her a heads-up." He mused for another minute, then turned to Zoe. "I'm not denying my relationship with Sam. Or with you. Have you thought about that?"

She hadn't, really. In all the recent uproar, she'd never once considered being in the news herself. "I think I need to sit down."

He led her to the steps. "Would Sam be able to keep it quiet if we asked him to? Only long enough to protect you, too, is all I'm thinking."

She thought, then shook her head. "Maybe, for a little while. But how do we explain why without making him feel bad?"

Will stared at her. "None of this is his fault, but you're right. Kylie and Sandra will just have to handle it the best they can." His look turned pleading. "Will you make sure he understands that I didn't know, either? I wouldn't have turned my back on him, Zoe, I swear. You don't have any reason to believe that, but I would like to think that I would have done the right thing."

Whatever his faults, Will Branch had always had a good heart. "I believe you. And I'm sorry that—"

He shook his head. "We can't go back. What happened, happened, but if we dwell on it, I'll go crazy. Tanner robbed me of too much." A muscle jumped in his jaw. He shook his head again, harder. "I can't." He looked at her. "You shouldn't, either. We're here now, and Sam is alive and healthy. We proceed from this point. Agreed?"

She nodded. There was a whole lot she didn't know about this new Will Branch, but so far, what she'd learned was promising.

Still, she wouldn't project too far or get her hopes up too high.

But she would give him a chance.

And be careful, in the process. "Agreed." She stuck out a hand.

Will took it and slowly drew her to him. Kissed the socks off her before she could protest. Even if she'd wanted to.

Then stepped back. "But I can do more than one thing at a time, honey. And you are on my radar screen, don't you forget it."

Flustered, flattered...altogether unsettled, Zoe escaped him as quickly as she could.

Before she went back for seconds and made a liar of herself.

MORNING LIGHT filtered through a gap at the side of the drapes. For a second, Zoe couldn't figure out where she was.

Then a small whisper. "Are you awake, Mom?"

She turned to see Sam, bright-eyed and ready, watching her as though he'd waited hours. "Hi, sweetie." She stretched. "How did you sleep?"

"Good." He bounced from the bed. "Can we go see Will?"

The previous night crashed in upon her, a kaleidoscope of locked horns and torrid kisses, of strong arms and comfort. Zoe sat up straight. "He might be sleeping."

"I don't think so. I peeked," he admitted. "He's working out."

Working out…oh, my. Thoughts of a sweaty Will made Zoe swallow hard. "I need to dress." Needed time. Distance.

"I'll wait out there," Sam offered, practically bubbling over with excitement.

"Let me grab a robe, then I have to ask Will about the shower. You need one, too, young man."

"Aw, mom, I had a spit bath last night." He wrinkled his nose. "Though I still think that's a gross thing to call it."

"That was my mother's term for a sponge bath." She smiled as she drew on her robe, then clutched it tightly at her throat. "Go ahead."

Sam yanked the door open, catching Will in the middle of a chin-up. He'd positioned a bar in brackets at the end of the short hallway leading to the living area. Both she and Sam stopped stock-still.

Lord have mercy, he looked…amazing. Clad only in a pair of gym shorts, his body was even more impressive than she'd imagined. An honest-to-goodness six-pack, arm and chest muscles bulging with his effort, long legs with rock-hard thighs and calves…oh, my.

A golden god was Mr. Will Branch. The lanky boy she'd made love with so long ago was somewhere inside this prime specimen, but…

The *good morning* she'd meant to say got stuck in her suddenly dry throat.

WILL DISMOUNTED and couldn't help doing a double take at the sight of Zoe in clinging silk, however closely she was gripping the opening of her robe. He wondered if she had a clue how beautiful she was, mussed and sleepy. How tantalizing her curves were beneath the thin fabric.

"Wow." Sam spoke and startled him. "You sure do work out, don't you?"

He tore his eyes from her and saw Sam comparing their arms. He knelt down in front of Sam. "Make a muscle." Sam complied hesitantly, and Will obligingly squeezed. "Yep, just as I thought."

"Terrible, huh?" Sam shrank.

"Nope. Just like me at your age."

"Really?"

"Cross my heart." And he did. "You've got plenty of time, if you decide you want to build muscles. You may not. You've got the only one that counts in tip-top shape."

Sam frowned. "I do?"

"Yep." Will tapped his temple. "That brain of yours is worth more than any ten men's arms and legs. Anyone can build a muscular body—only takes hard work and discipline. I'm thinking that you have both of those skills mastered, based on what your mom tells me about how you do in school. I work out because it helps my driving. Five hundred laps in a car at high speeds takes a lot of control and stamina, so I perform better if I'm strong. You may want to go into something else. You'll always want to keep your body healthy, but you might prefer to be a runner or a swimmer or a cyclist. Strength is important, but there are all kinds of strength."

"I want to be strong like you," Sam insisted.

Will rose. Dared to check Zoe's expression, which, he was relieved to see, was approving. "Well, you've got a few years to decide. I was built a lot like you when I was your age, and I was still pretty skinny back when I knew your mother—just ask her."

Sam swiveled his head. Zoe nodded. "He's much more…" Her voice was husky, and Will had to turn away before the effect on him was visible. "Muscular."

Will grabbed the towel he'd been using to wipe off sweat. Walked toward the other end of the motor home. "Hope I didn't wake you all. I didn't use the weights because they clank, but I can't afford to let my conditioning slide." He didn't face them yet. Realized he was nervous in Zoe's presence. To buy time, he swigged more water from his bottle.

"You didn't wake us, at least not me," Zoe said. "Um, is it okay to shower? I wasn't sure if there's a limit on the water or…" Her voice faded, but Will barely noticed, caught as he was by the image of Zoe in his shower.

Holy hell. How did dads do it? Deal with their children's sexy mothers when the kids were present and not embarrass everyone?

He was the one who needed a shower. Ice-cold. "Go ahead. There should be plenty. Mike's got us hooked up, and the water heater's good-sized." If she left, maybe he could just stand outside in the cold air and bring his unruly body under control.

Zoe hesitated, drawing his attention. Her eyes seemed to telegraph a question. *Wait for me,* she mouthed.

He nodded, understanding that she referred to telling Sam. As if he'd do it without her. "Hey, bud," he said to Sam. "You hungry?"

Sam nodded, fair hair bouncing. "I can help."

Will stroked his head, smiling. "Well, that's good, since we could starve to death if I have to be the cook. I can do a mean bowl of cereal, though."

"I like cereal," Sam said.

Will bent to him with a stage whisper. "I mostly have to eat healthy to keep up my conditioning, but I have some Froot Loops stashed away for special occasions. Interested?"

Sam cut a glance toward Zoe, who rolled her eyes but smiled. "Go ahead," she said. "This one time."

Sam's grin was morning sunshine. "Sure!"

"I'll get you set up, then I've got fifty more push-ups calling my name."

"Fifty? Wow!"

Will grinned. He'd been working out so long it had lost its luster. Mostly it was just a necessary grind.

But Sam's reaction made him proud, and Will liked that feeling. A lot. "Maybe you could count them for me while you're lolling around and eating," he teased.

"I could do that. I'm really good at math, you know."

Will gave him a quick hug. A startled Sam hesitated, then gripped him tightly around his waist and held on.

Touched to his core, Will renewed his grip and let Sam be the one to let go first.

He'd never done push-ups before with a lump in his throat, but he had a feeling he was in for a lot of firsts now.

BY TACIT AGREEMENT, Will and Zoe exchanged places once she'd dressed. She sat and chatted with Sam while Will took a quick shower and grabbed a clean uniform, then rejoined them.

It was hard not to be proud when he saw Sam's admiring gaze. The boy had it bad for racing, no question. Will only hoped that he'd still be feeling so positive at the end of this conversation.

He took advantage of Sam's turned back to whisper to Zoe, "Let me start, okay?"

She seemed startled and not all that convinced, but he plunged ahead, unwilling to be a coward. He would tell the truth and see if they'd all survive it. He wanted an honest relationship with his son. "Sam, there's something your mom and I need to tell you."

Sam turned, his expression both quizzical and anxious. "What is it?"

"Come here, okay?" Will drew him to a seat at the small dining table.

"Is it bad?"

Will smiled. "I don't think so. I hope you won't, either, but if it helps, I'm more nervous than you."

Sam's eyes popped. "You?"

Will nodded. "Me. So I'm just going to talk man-to-man. All right?"

The mop of blond hair shook with Sam's nod.

Every word in Will's carefully-prepared shower speech vaporized from his head. He frowned. "What do you know about how babies get made?"

Zoe's quiet gasp told him he'd found the wrong ones. Sam shrugged. "Some of my friends talk about the sex thing, but it sounds kinda gross."

Will stifled a smile. "It did to me, too, at your age. All I can tell you is that things change. Sex with someone you care about can be pretty wonderful." Sam's expression showed his doubts. Will plunged ahead. "But that's not the point, except to say that, well, sometimes people have sex when they're not married. Like your mom and me when we were younger."

Sam's horrified glance shot to Zoe, who was looking as if she'd like to murder him. "Will—"

"He needs to know. He's too smart to pass off with babyish answers. Right, Sam?"

"I guess."

"I was really crazy about your mom, and she was pretty stuck on me, too. Maybe we should have waited to make love, but we didn't." A thought occurred. "We were out of high school, though. We tried to be careful, but your mom got pregnant, only I didn't know. I knew you were born, but I had no idea you were mine. If I had, I would have been with you long before."

Sam frowned. "I'm…yours? Your son?"

When Sam's eyes widened, Will probably should have

waited, but he couldn't. "Yes. I'm your father, Sam. I don't know if you like that idea, but I do. I really do. I'm just sorry I didn't know before. I would have liked to see you when you were little. That's not to say—" he hastily amended and felt all thumbs as Sam leaned back, his eyes filling with tears "—that I don't like who you are now. I do, Sam. I like you a lot. I know you thought Tanner was your dad and maybe you're sorry that I—"

He didn't get a chance to continue, as sixty pounds of child slammed into his chest, and skinny arms hung on hard. Will looked helplessly at Zoe, whose eyes were wet, too, then he returned his attention to Sam. "Does this mean you're all right with it?"

Sam drew back for an instant, though he didn't let go. "You're my dad, really?" His eyes searched Will's. "You're not just saying that?"

"I'm not, I promise. I don't know much about being a dad, so you might have to teach me, but—oof!" Sam gripped him again with surprising strength, and all Will knew to do was hang on. He lowered his cheek to Sam's head. "So it's really okay with you?" he murmured.

The small headed nodded. "Can I call you Dad?" he asked softly.

"You bet you can." Something inside Will tore loose, some wall of uncertainty that had bottled up feelings that flooded through him now. *Let me be enough,* he thought. *Let me be the father this boy needs.* Throat tight, he lifted his head and saw Zoe's tears flowing unchecked. He also spotted the worry she couldn't quite hide and saw maybe even a trace of the love they had once shared.

He didn't know how he was going to balance everything he needed to, how to fight Zoe's doubts and his own while maintaining the focus and drive that would make him a champion. His career was not yet stellar enough to buy him future security. The star drivers got the endorsements, made money through many different avenues and invested it to secure their futures after their racing careers ended.

Will wasn't there, wasn't even close. He'd been living for the moment, relishing the life of a NASCAR driver with no thought for tomorrow. He'd had ambition aplenty, but it had extended no further than being a champion.

Now he had a child. And, if he were lucky, a woman—but he would not have her if he couldn't demonstrate that he could be a lot more than he had been. He wanted to provide for them, to secure a future for all of them. That meant whole-sale changes in his life at a time when the pressures on him as a driver were enormous. One false step, and he'd lose his ride—and he was suited for nothing else. Never wanted to be anything else. His father had stolen the trust fund that had allowed Will to be stupid and callow, to live for today and blow off tomorrow. He had no practical job skills, and now someone besides Will Branch needed him to be not only a breadwin-ner but a good example, a source of strength and comfort.

He was scared as hell that he wasn't up to the task.

But the boy in his arms deserved better. The woman who'd brought this boy to him did, too. For better or worse, they would see what Will Branch was made of, all of them.

Sam squeezed him again, then stepped back. "So if you're my dad, do I get to be a Branch?" His look grew resolute. "I'm not a Hitchens anymore, right, Mom? Neither are you."

Zoe sank into her chair. "There's a lot to be decided, sweetheart."

"Are we going to live with you?" he asked Will.

"You don't mess around, do you?" Will found a chuckle, despite his discomfort. "Listen, champ, I don't have all the answers and neither does your mom. You all live in Dallas, and I'm on the road most of the year."

"We could travel with you."

"Sam," Zoe protested, "you have school."

"Some kids get homeschooled," he insisted. "You could

do that. You're smart." He turned to Will. "Couldn't I, Dad? Ryan told me yesterday that some drivers' kids do that."

"Tell you what, sport." Will resisted pointing out to Zoe that he'd suggested the same thing. "Let's just go do some testing today and figure this out one step at a time, okay? It's a big change for all of us."

"You don't really want me." Sam's voice turned dull.

Will grasped his arms and looked him in the eye. "That is absolutely not true. I want you very much. I'm proud of you, proud to be seen with you. But your mom has a different life, and she might not want to be dragged around all over the country. Trust me, it's not as exciting as it seems. It gets really old." He smiled. "We've got some time during the off-season to come up with answers. Work with us, okay? We'll figure things out, I promise."

"I think it would be cool."

Will got his first taste of dealing with a boy with a stubborn streak. He couldn't help thinking that his mother would be very amused, considering Will's own. "School's important, bud. Let's think about trying out traveling in the summer, maybe." He cast a glance at Zoe. "If it's okay with your mom."

He could see the protest forming, and tried a quick feint. "But for now, how about we go tell Mike?"

Sam's eyes lit. "Yeah! Let's go, Dad." He grabbed Will's hand and practically dragged him to the door.

"You coming, Zoe?" Will asked.

She was frowning at him. He'd done the best he could, but it was obviously not enough.

"I'll catch up with you both in a few minutes. You mind your manners, Sam."

"I will." Sam was out the door like a shot, and all Will could do was follow.

CHAPTER TEN

TWO DAYS BEFORE CHRISTMAS, Zoe's stomach was tied up in knots as she wrapped yet another package for a family member she'd never met. Sam had been introduced to all of Will's family but the youngest brother, Sawyer, and his girlfriend, Lucy, but Zoe had stayed away from them on purpose. Not that the Branches weren't nice people—no one was kinder than Maeve Branch—but they were Sam's family, not hers. Not that Sam hadn't hinted daily how much he'd like her and Will and himself to be a unit. But Sam was living in a dreamworld right now.

Ever since they'd returned from Halesboro, Will had been very much in evidence. He called every morning to talk to Sam before he left for school, and he met the bus nearly every afternoon. Weekends, he spirited Sam away to an arcade or to the nearby speedway, even though racing was on hiatus. He'd finagled one of the racing school cars with a passenger seat and taken Sam for laps around the track that Sam was still talking about.

If there was a person on the planet who didn't know that Sam was Will Branch's son, it was only because Sam hadn't met that person yet. He figured out a way to work that fact into nearly every conversation. Both Will and Bart had been surprised that the press hadn't picked up the story yet, but Kylie had credited the holidays and told them their luck wouldn't hold forever. Will's sponsors had been informed of the situation, but the combination of a detailed explanation and Will's obvious pride in Sam appeared to have eased their concerns. Everyone seemed prepared to put the best spin on it, though Zoe couldn't help worrying.

Will had also taken Sam to spend the night at the Branch mansion twice. Zoe had been invited, assured there was plenty of room and that she was welcome, but she'd demurred, citing the need to catch up on various chores when in reality, something she'd have once dreamed of— time alone to pamper herself—had turned into hours that dragged until Sam came back home.

Sam was in kid heaven. Will seemed pleased as punch. He'd taken to fatherhood like a duck to water—

Except that he hadn't, really. He was on vacation, and he made every day a vacation for Sam.

Being a parent was not about being a playmate, or certainly not all the time. Will had yet to get a taste of true fatherhood. Zoe did the disciplining—not that Sam needed much right now, when he was getting everything he'd ever dreamed of—and she made sure he ate right, did his homework, although, to be fair, Will was much better at math than she was and had taken over that chore.

But the salient fact that kept Zoe awake at night was the knowledge that Will wasn't racing. Aside from some sponsor obligations at holiday events, he had all the time in the world to devote to spoiling his son.

He was doing a good job of it, and when Zoe tried to rein him in, neither he nor Sam listened.

But the reckoning would come. The season would begin, and she knew exactly how much Will's focus would shift. Hadn't she experienced it firsthand?

It would kill Sam. Not that Will didn't mean well. Zoe believed he honestly loved his son.

So she held herself apart from their infatuation with each other and tried to prepare herself to catch Sam when inevitably the fall came. When Will's attention turned once again to the track. To the world that had claimed him long before she or Sam had existed for him. She also kept a tight rein on her own feelings about Will, and the potent attraction he wielded for her.

The knock on her front door yanked Zoe out of her thoughts, and she frowned. Sam was out of school and on another overnighter with Will. She wasn't expecting any visitors. Clad in ancient jeans and a fleece top along with her fuzzy slippers, she was hardly prepared.

Another knock. She crossed to the peephole and peered out.

Yanked the door open. "What's wrong? Where's Sam?"

Will stood there, looking too blasted sexy for his own good in black slacks and a blue sweater that brought out the color of his eyes. "Nothing's wrong. Sam's fine." He smiled and proffered a bouquet from behind his back.

Violets. Not at all easy to find this time of year, and her favorite.

She didn't accept them. "Where is he? Why isn't he with you?"

Will stepped across the threshold and stroked her cheek with the blossoms. "Playing Grand Theft Auto with Bart and Sawyer."

"Will, he can't—" That game was violent and absolutely forbidden.

Will grinned. "Kidding. They're playing a new game I got him—not violent, Mom. Or at least not enough that I'd be in trouble."

She didn't press the issue. She was trying not to be a control freak and give Will a chance. "Why are you here, then?"

"For this." He leaned in and kissed her. Kissed her good. When she tried to unscramble her thoughts and draw away, he slid one arm around her and kicked the door shut with his foot, taking his time to let the kiss spool out to devastating effect.

She was the approximate texture of overcooked pasta when he finally came up for air. Touched his forehead to hers. "Gotta stop. I swore I'd take you out on a real date, even if what I really want to do is take you straight to bed."

"Will—" She sidestepped. "I'm not dressed."

"Unfortunately," he drawled. "You are."

"I…I…what if I have plans?"

"I hope you'll cancel them. Or work me in." Those killer blue eyes were as magnetic as his thoroughly wicked smile. "Want me to wait?" He strolled over to the sofa and plopped down, splaying his arms along the back. "Go ahead. I'm at your mercy."

She frowned. "Will, you can't just—"

"Would you have said yes if I'd asked you out?" He shook his head. "Don't bother lying. I'm getting tired of being rejected." His lips curved. "It's bad for my confidence."

"Like you aren't cocky enough for a dozen men," she muttered.

He sat forward. "Let me take you out, Zoe, please. Just for dinner." His brows rose hopefully. "We have Sam's blessing."

It was so hard to remember what she knew was real when he was playful like this. Will Branch could charm the birds from the trees when he wanted to. She had to keep herself apart from him in order to be there for Sam when the inevitable disappointment came.

"I can't."

"Can't?" One brow arched. "Or won't?" He sobered completely. "He keeps asking me for only one thing, Zoe. He likes all the gifts, yeah, but you know what he wants, the only thing he really wants in the world?"

She did. She heard the litany often. "Sam has to learn that life doesn't always grant your wishes."

"He could have this one, if you'd let him."

"No, Will." However much appeal there was to Sam's idea of being a family, the three of them, Will had devastated her once, and she wasn't taking chances with her child's heart. "I…I want other things from life." It was the best defense she could muster—even if it wasn't completely true. But until she saw just how Will balanced his career and family, she would use whatever was at hand.

His eyes darkened, seeming almost…hurt? No, not cocky Will Branch.

Predictably, he rallied. "I'll keep asking."

"You'll get the same answer."

"One day you'll believe in me, Zoe." Frustration simmered, but he kept his temper. He did an about-face. "But tonight, just come to dinner with me. You have to eat, right?"

"I'll be seeing you—and your whole family—in two days." She'd agreed to spend the night on Christmas Eve so Sam could experience the entire family holiday. Sam was ecstatic, and she was actually looking forward to it herself—if only expectations weren't part of the package. She couldn't hurt Maeve Branch by discussing her lack of faith in Maeve's son. She would simply have to get through it the best she could, as a treat for her child.

He flashed a grin. "Mom's putting you in my room."

Her mouth dropped open. "She is not!"

He laughed. "Well, I could ask. Mom would do most anything for the son who provided her with Sam." He grew serious. "She's absolutely crazy about him, and he's really taken to her."

"Your mother is a lovely person. I would have adored having a grandmother like her."

His look said that she could be part of them at any time, but thankfully, he didn't press the issue. "So don't make me disappoint her by coming home too soon. She has designs on Sam. Even if it means learning to play video games with him. They made a trade—he's baking Christmas cookies with her and she's trying out a game controller." He shook his head. "Mom's hopeless with video games, but Sam doesn't give up as easily as we did."

Zoe had to grin at the image of elegant Maeve Branch sitting on the floor in front of a TV screen. "She's wonderful."

"So are you. She thinks the world of your mothering skills. Says she wished she could have made us behave half so well, even once."

Zoe flushed. "Thank you for telling me that."

"I'll tell you more over dinner. Come with me, Zoe? Please?" He took her fingers and pressed a kiss to them.

A long evening with nothing to do stretched out before her. "All right. But I have to change."

"I could help." His brows waggled lasciviously.

Zoe couldn't stem a chuckle. "You wish." As she left the room, she heard him sigh.

"You'd better believe it."

She was smiling as she closed the bedroom door between them.

Before she yielded to temptation and invited him in.

DINNER WAS A REVELATION. Will Branch could behave himself. Their relationship had been so intense all those years ago and the stakes had been so high since Tanner had died that the art of simple conversation without tension was a new experience.

"You surprise me," she said after he brought up a book she would never have expected him to read.

"You think I only read about motor sports?"

"No, of course not." But she had thought that.

"I have a lot of hours to kill on the road. The season can get pretty intense, even one without all the upheaval of this one. I have to get away from it for a while." Then his lips curved. "So you thought I, what, played video games all the time?"

"You used to."

"I used to be a stupid kid, Zoe." He leaned toward her. "I'm grown up now." His voice was husky, his eyes warm Caribbean waters. "In case you hadn't noticed."

How could she not? She swallowed hard. "Will…"

A flash of white teeth, then he settled back, his expression satisfied. "Okay, I'm done." His eyebrows waggled. "For the moment. So tell me about Sam's life," he said in a lightning switch of topic.

"What do you want to know?"

"No detail is too small. When did he learn to ride a bike?" A line appeared between his brows. "He does ride, right? 'Cause I was looking at this BMX he would go nuts over."

"Will, you can't—" She sighed. "You can spoil him, of course, but that's not what he wants from you."

"And it's not all I want, either. I want time with him, more than anything. But is it so wrong to want to make up for all the time we've lost? What's the point of busting my buns out on the track if I can't take care of my boy?"

"But—"

"Does he have a bike, Zoe? Does he like riding one?" Will raked his fingers through his hair. "I hate that I don't know these things."

Guilt rode her hard, but so did compassion. "You have time now, Will." She placed her hand over his. *If you'll take it,* she thought, but didn't say out loud.

He turned his palm up and interlaced their fingers. Heaved a sigh. "I'll try to slow down. I promise. But he's such a great kid, and there's so much I want to do for him. So much ground to cover." The pain in his eyes undid her.

"I'm sorry," she said, and meant it.

He squeezed her fingers and lifted them to his lips. "Me, too. This isn't easy on you, and I don't want that." He sat up straighter. Released her. "So…tell me about his first tooth."

He surprised her. He confused her.
Most of all, he touched her.
Even if she didn't want him to.

CHAPTER ELEVEN

ON CHRISTMAS EVE MORNING, Will was up bright and early, working out with unusual fervor. He'd been tempted to skip it, but he needed to chill out. He was far too amped up over having Zoe and Sam with his family for three days and two nights.

Zoe had argued that one night was plenty—more than she wanted, he knew—but Mom, bless her, had made a convincing case for a new tradition she wanted to begin in her first year with Chuck, having story time around the Christmas tree on Christmas night. Each family member would tell a story from his or her past, and that way they would all get to know each other, this blended family.

One of Chuck's sons and his family were here, in addition to Bart, Will's younger brother, Sawyer, and his girlfriend, Lucy, sister, Penny, her husband, Craig, and baby Diane, whom they'd named after Maeve's mother. And, of course, Harry, his mom's dog whom Sam adored. The house would be full to bursting once Zoe and Sam arrived, and Mom was in seventh heaven.

Will felt a little like a kid before Christmas himself, eager to pick them up now instead of 10:00 a.m., as Zoe had finally agreed.

She wasn't making things easy on him, but he found himself not pushing as much as he'd like to, either. The balance with Zoe was so delicate…the slightest scare would send her running, he was sure.

Which was why, despite his intentions, he hadn't pushed her to make love when they'd returned to her apartment after dinner the other night. Not that he hadn't wanted to—being with Zoe consumed far too much of his attention, and that wasn't likely to change. Especially not when he could still hear her breathy little moans, feel her slender fingers digging into his flesh as they lost themselves in yet another scorching kiss—

"You're going to hurt yourself, dumbass." Bart strolled into the home gym. "Lifting that much without a spotter." He took a post at Will's head, his expression sour.

"Up yours," Will said with a grin. Nothing could foul up his mood this morning.

"You're awful cheery." Bart winced as the weights clanked.

"I wasn't out partying half the night."

"Yeah, why, exactly, was that? The redhead was asking for you. Real put out that you left early." Bart's expression turned calculating. "Becoming a dad has changed you."

"I think it's supposed to." Will rose, wiped his face with a towel. "At least, with a dad who gives a crap."

"Dad cared about us, you know. It wasn't all bad."

"What, you're forgiving him now?"

Bart shrugged. "It's Christmas. He's in jail, all alone."

Will goggled. "Well, you can get soft on him if you want, but not me. Being with Sam changes everything, makes me madder than ever that the old man only wanted us for show ponies. I'll never do that to my boy. Never."

"He's a terrific little guy." Bart shook his head. "I still can't get used to you having a son. I guess I thought it would be years before either of us got married." He glanced over. "How's it going with Zoe?"

"Slow." Will grinned. "But I'm wearing away at her."

"You think so? That's what you want, the package deal?"

"It's what's best for Sam." Will sobered. "She doesn't trust me, though."

Bart snorted. "Imagine that."

Will ignored his brother. "She thinks I'll flake out when the season starts, but I won't."

"You so sure? The guys with families have to juggle a lot. You positive you're up to it?"

Will admitted to his twin what he steadfastly denied to Zoe. "I honestly don't know." He stared at the floor for a long time. Then he looked up. "But I have to figure it out somehow. I can't give up racing—like I know how to do anything else—and I'm not giving up Sam. He's had it rough. So has Zoe. If I could just get her to see that it can work—"

Bart clapped him on the shoulder. "I'll do what I can, you know that." He turned playful again, waggled his eyebrows. "Need me to woo your woman for you?"

Will slugged him on the shoulder. "Not in this lifetime." He settled back on the bench. Talk of the season was making him nervous. He had so much to prove—to the racing world, as well as to Zoe. "Add twenty pounds to each side, and let's rock."

"You got a death wish, dude?"

Will took a deep breath and gripped the bar. "Nope. Just getting ready to kick your butt on the track."

Bart smirked. "In your dreams." But he loaded the plates onto the bar and settled back to spot his brother.

ZOE HANDED Will two shopping bags full of wrapped presents, gifts she'd agonized over for his family. She'd had to use her ingenuity, since she didn't have funds to spare, and she wished yet again she'd had more time and knew all of them better. Maybe they'd hate the homemade gifts she and Sam had labored over.

"What?" Will watched her too closely. "You're worrying again. Please don't, Zoe. No one's going to bite you, I swear."

"It's not that. It's just…" She'd done her best to make holidays special for Sam, but at the moment she thought she'd take the cold, formal occasions at the Hitchenses' mansion over the uncertainties she faced now. Sam was part of Will's family, but she wasn't. Didn't want to be, she reminded herself, but she was little more than an interloper—excess baggage—when what everyone really wanted was Sam.

"Come here." Will set down the bags and drew her close. "What are you afraid of, sweetheart?"

This. Exactly this. How good it feels right here in your arms. "Nothing," she said against his shirt front.

"Zoe." His voice was husky. Intimate. She knew, absolutely knew that if she lingered, he would kiss her.

He was getting tougher and tougher to resist.

She drew back quickly. "It's just nerves," she said briskly, upset with herself for displaying weakness. "You have the suitcase with his gifts from Santa?" Sam didn't really believe in Santa anymore, but he didn't push the issue. She suspected he wasn't any more ready than her to give it up.

"Safely stashed." He regarded her. "What can I do to make this easier?"

"I'm fine." He looked dubious. "Ready?" Nothing would be solved by lagging. She just had to go on, so she could get this over with. Put the holidays behind them and get back to their routines.

Then see how much those routines would change. See if Will would change.

While she was busy thinking, Will swooped down and planted a sound kiss on her mouth.

"What was that for?"

He stroked one finger down the line between her brows and grinned. "To bolster you for the trip to the gas chamber. One last kiss for the condemned woman and all that." His blue eyes twinkled, and she couldn't quite catch her breath, the way he was looking at her.

"I'm not that bad," she protested.

"Coulda fooled me." He winked. "After you, madam."

Sam charged back from Will's car just then. "Mom, are you ready yet?" Impatience oozed from his every pore.

Zoe smiled and smoothed one hand over his hair. "I'm ready."

Or not. Regardless, here I come.

WILL HAD WATCHED her all day, observed her hanging back at first. She was like a doe afraid to move toward the pond, however desperate she might be for a drink of water.

His family was having none of it. He'd never been prouder of them. Little Diane had been the key; she'd reached for Zoe when Zoe had been introduced to Penny and Craig, and Penny had kindly relinquished her. Zoe's face had literally glowed, charmed by the baby girl who'd enraptured the entire Branch family, and Will had actually had a second of imagining himself and Zoe with a second child.

That he hadn't run the instant the thought had occurred should have scared him half to death. He didn't even know how to deal with one child who was half grown and independent. What was he doing, even thinking about babies he and Zoe could make?

First things first. Having babies necessitated making love, and he was a long way from accomplishing that—though maybe not so far as before, given the warm looks Zoe was giving him now and again.

Of course, she was giving his whole family more smiles than she'd ever granted him. Bart had her playing video games with him and Sam, and Zoe was so much looser with his brother than she was with him. She'd engaged in long discussions of child-rearing with Penny and his mom, and she'd pitched in to help Gerty and his mom cook.

They'd attended candlelight services, and he'd been mesmerized by Zoe in the golden glow. He'd been proud to stand with his son at one side and Zoe at the other, his heart full of a feeling he'd never known before.

Could he really be falling in love with Zoe? It felt different from before—yes, there was still the physical aspect, and sometimes he remembered only too well how he'd thought back then that he'd die if he couldn't have her.

He felt that way now, but there was something beyond. He yearned for Zoe, always would, he guessed, but he found himself wishing for the quieter moments, too, like later in the evening, when she'd let him read *The Night Before Christmas* to Sam at bedtime, part of their holiday tradition. When she and he had faced each other across their son's bed, on that most magical of nights for a child. They'd put Sam to bed together, and it had been an intimacy different from any he'd ever experienced, one that tangled up in his heart and sank roots he was pretty sure he'd never extricate.

Or want to.

So here he was, tossing in his childhood room, unable to sleep. Only it wasn't visions of what might be underneath the Christmas tree that taunted him.

It was visions of Zoe.

Finally, he shoved himself up from the bed, grabbed a pair of sweats and put them on, padding down the stairs in stocking feet. He considered watching some TV, but he wasn't interested in the outside world. Instead, he headed for his mother's conservatory.

Only to discover that someone else had beaten him there. Zoe. Curled up asleep on the wicker sofa, bare feet peeking from beneath the afghan his mother kept nearby in winter.

God, she was beautiful, never more so than like this, hair loose and tangled, face clean of makeup, just…Zoe.

Will started to sit in a nearby chair but instead yielded to temptation and sank to the floor in front of her.

I could watch this face for hours, he thought. For years, he suspected. He studied every line of her features with a thoroughness that would have had her squirming if she'd been awake.

Resisted, just barely, tracing them with his fingers.

When her eyes opened, pupils dark with slumber, he resisted no longer and bent forward to press his lips to her own.

"Mmm," she hummed, deep in her throat.

So he slid his tongue over the seam. Teased entrance inside, to the warm sweetness of her mouth. He tunneled one hand into her hair and slanted to deepen the kiss.

"Will?" She awoke then. "What—"

"Shh," he soothed, and stretched out beside her, one hand slipping over her shoulder, tracing the dip of her waist, the flare of her hips and around to her back, bringing her belly to his.

A quick intake of air, her body against his had his pulse racing and need gnawing at his self-control. *Come to my bed,* he started to say, but he was afraid he'd lose her in the time required to ascend the stairs and get to his room.

The house slept around them, and the plants created a bower to hide them. He forced himself not to press against her as his fevered body was begging him to do, but when his fingers reached the hem of her nightgown and touched her flesh, his control barely held.

He gripped her so tightly he wondered if she could breathe, while he fought back his instinct to make her his once more.

"What's wrong?"

"Just give me a minute." He could hear the strain in his voice and knew she must.

She froze, as well. Bit her lush lower lip. He wanted to lick at the sharp edges of her teeth, soothe the discomfort. "I want you so damn much."

Her eyes were wide and dark and knowing. Sultry. "Me, too."

"Yeah?" He hesitated. "It has to be both of us, Zoe. I'll never force you."

"I know." She paused, as well. "It's just—"

He closed his eyes, cursing himself for being too reasonable. So damn noble, when his body was clawed bloody by the need of her.

"I'm such a coward," she whispered. "No more," she said fiercely. "I don't want to think, Will. Don't want to worry all the time. Is it so wrong to want, just this once, only to feel?"

"I won't hurt you, Zoe, I swear it."

"You will," she said. "I know you will, but I don't want to care. Not tonight."

He readied himself to argue that she was wrong.

But one small hand gripped his waist, then burrowed beneath his T-shirt and stroked up his side.

And every last word fled his mind.

"You are so built," she said, as she caressed him, played over his chest as though he were her own private toy. "All these muscles drive me crazy."

Will couldn't believe what he was hearing. Zoe, wanting him. Hot for him. He wanted to shout for joy. Promise her anything.

He would not hurt her. She didn't believe him, but she'd see.

Then her mouth began to follow the rising hem of his shirt, pressing slow kisses over his belly and driving him not so slowly out of his mind. "Zoe, babe," he groaned. "You have to stop. I've wanted you too long. I'm too close—"

She paused in her torture and flashed an evil grin, shocking him speechless. One eyebrow arched. "Make me."

Will stared at her. Didn't try to find his voice.

Focused instead on sweeping her up and carrying her to his room. Distracting her along the way until she writhed in his arms. Settling her in his bed and focusing only on her until she murmured tiny, breathy cries, torturing her with hot kisses, sweet caresses and teasing touches until she was quivering, strung tight with need for him as powerful as his own.

Until she was so gone that, at long last, he could go with her.

And if he thought he heard *I love you,* he wasn't sure if it was coming from Zoe's lips or his own. Maybe both.

All he knew was that Christmas had arrived early for him.

And he wanted it to stay forever.

IT WAS A LITTLE SURREAL to not be sitting in her robe watching Sam open presents on Christmas morning but to instead be fully dressed—especially when all the Branches were decidedly casual in their attire. She was company, though, not family, and there was no way she could sit around comfortably in her nightgown and robe in front of virtual strangers.

It was a whole lot more surreal to be sitting right beside Will, squirming at how she'd lost her mind in his arms only hours before. She peeked at Maeve, wondering if the truth was written on her face. In scarlet, no less.

"You're blushing," Will said, bending near.

"Stop it." She glanced at him—the devastating grin, the cleft in his chin she'd licked—*licked!*—the night before. She forced her attention away, clasping her fingers so tightly her knuckles went white.

Will chuckled, sounding all too much like a very satisfied male.

Bart looked up from where Sam was demonstrating how his new chemistry set worked, and his eyes flicked from Will to her and back. He ducked his head, grinning, and Zoe longed to jam her elbow into Will's side.

But that would only attract more attention. Heaven help

her, she'd committed to be here another night, when just at this moment, she wanted to run from the house screaming.

She'd almost made love with Will in his mother's conservatory, for Pete's sake, before moving to his room. Anyone could have caught them. She was mortified, horrified, scandalized—

But oh, how she shivered at the memories, too numerous—and delicious—to count. He'd been everything she'd imagined—and more. Mercy...so much more.

She jumped up and moved toward the tree. "May I help you, Sam?" she asked in a voice too high to be her own.

"We can both help you, son," a deep voice said from behind her.

"Go away," she hissed softly.

"Not on your life, honey."

Zoe swallowed hard and picked up a present, then realized it was the one she'd made for Will. "Here." She all but shoved it in his belly. "Go open your present."

"Who's it from?" He examined the tag, then looked at her with honest surprise. "For me?"

Everyone was watching them, and Zoe was near tears from humiliation. She was sure every single person—children excepted—knew what they'd done last night. "It's nothing. No big deal. Please—" She begged him with her eyes. "Please go away."

He frowned, then nodded. Walked back to his seat slowly.

Zoe turned back to the tree, crouching so she'd be less noticeable. "Here, Sam. Would you please take this to Mr. Lawrence?"

"Chuck, please," the older man said. "We're family, after all."

But I'm not, she wanted to protest. *I can't be.* Even if last night had made her dream of things she had no right wishing for. "Chuck," she agreed, just to get along.

She busied herself digging out gifts and handing them to

Sam, noticing, in the process, that her child's stack was by far the largest. "Let me finish, sweetheart, and you go ahead and open yours. Want to?"

Eagerly Sam agreed. He dove into his stack, and she admired each gift even as she despaired of the bounty she would never be able to match. "Wow!" was followed by "Cool!" and "Awesome!" Thoroughly comfortable with all of them, Sam ran from one to the next, throwing his arms around each giver and regaling them with all the wonders of each gift. The room was filled with happy people, especially Maeve, who'd gotten teary over the grandmother brag book Zoe had assembled for her, filled with pictures of Sam.

In the midst of the melee, Zoe finally noticed that Will had gone utterly silent. She squirmed more than ever at her choice of gifts for him, but she had to return to his side to open her own stack of gifts. She walked slowly, as if to her own execution.

Will looked up at her approach, and she was shocked to her marrow to see his eyes moist. "Thank you," he said in a husky voice. "This is the best present I ever got, except for Sam himself." He laid his hand on the scrapbook she'd made for him detailing Sam's life from birth to now, taking some of her treasured mementoes such as Sam's drawings, cards he'd made, report cards, a lock of baby hair, along with photos from every age.

"I…I figured you could buy anything you really wanted, but this was something you couldn't obtain for yourself. A small way to give you back what Tanner stole from you."

Will reached for her hand, squeezed it. "Thank you. I don't know what to say." He reached into his pocket and drew out a small box.

Zoe froze.

"Don't look so horrified. It's not a ring. I wouldn't do that to you." He leaned closer. "Not that I didn't consider it."

She didn't respond to the last but unwrapped it with

unsteady fingers, aware that on some level she was disappointed, however absurd the notion of marriage to Will was.

Then she gasped. A heart-shaped locket very much like the one he'd won for her at the carnival.

Only this one was real. And expensive. "Oh, Will…"

"Open it."

The other one had held a picture of the two of them. She was a little afraid to see what was in here, but when she at last got it open, she smiled, deeply moved.

It was Sam and Will together, mugging for the camera.

"This is beautiful, Will. Thank you so much."

He opened his mouth to respond, but just then, Sam charged across the room, throwing his arms around Will's neck. "Dad, thanks! Wow, my own uniform! Look, Mom, it's just like Dad's!"

Will hugged Sam back hard, closing his eyes as he did, as though savoring his child's embrace.

Zoe had to turn away then or cry for sure. At that moment, her eyes met Maeve's, and Will's mother beamed and blew her a kiss. *Thank you,* she mouthed.

Zoe tried to smile, but emotions swamped her, and she rushed from the room.

Maeve followed her. "Can I do anything?"

Zoe didn't turn but only shook her head. "I'm sorry. You're wonderful. This is—" She fluttered her hands. "Everyone is so good to Sam, and you've been kind to include me. I really appreciate it, I just—"

Maeve touched her shoulder, turned her gently. "May I?" She held out her arms, and Zoe knew it would be so easy to accept the mother's love Maeve offered so freely.

She stepped forward, then back. "No. It wouldn't be fair."

"Why?"

"Because I can't…Will isn't…" She gave up. "I'm not family, and I can't pretend."

"Could you let me be your friend?" Maeve asked. "I

know there's a lot for you and Will to work out, but I see the happiness on my son's face, and I can't help wanting him to have more of it. The last year has been very difficult for all my children, but Will and Bart had to deal not only with their father's betrayal personally but professionally. They've been fighting for their lives in racing while trying to deal with a father who abandoned them. That's tough at any age, and Will's mischievous manner has always been his way to hide a very tender heart. He's suffered, and I was too much a mess for months to help him. You make him happy, Zoe, and I can't help wanting that for him."

She shook her head vigorously. "Sam makes him happy, not me."

"Sam does make him very happy—he already adores that child—but I see how he looks at you."

"No. It won't work. Besides, racing takes up most of his time now."

Maeve pursed her lips. "I don't know about that. I do agree that racing can be all-consuming—"

"Can be and is. I know that better than anyone. I'm sorry, Mrs. Branch—I mean, Mrs. Lawrence—"

"Maeve, sweetheart." Maeve took her hand, pressed it between her own. "May I ask you this one favor, please?"

"What's that?"

"Will you give my son a chance? Racing does take an enormous amount of a driver's life, but there are drivers who manage to balance racing and family. I've met them. As a matter of fact, I'd like to introduce you to Patsy Grosso. She and I have become friends over the years, and she's had to deal with not only a husband but a son who are drivers."

Zoe stiffened. "I don't want Sam to get involved with racing."

Maeve smiled softly. "I can't say that I wanted Will and Bart to do so, either, but at the end of the day, isn't what we want most for our children is that they be fulfilled in whatever they choose to do?"

Zoe stiffened. "Mrs.—Maeve, I don't want to sound—"

Maeve shook her head. "It's I who should apologize. You've come here under duress, and I'm adding to the pressures you're feeling. Please, let me back up and say that I do want to be your friend, honestly, and I think I'm capable of being so, even if you and my son can't work out a future together." She squeezed Zoe's hand. "We will forever be linked by Sam, and that sweet child deserves the best all of us have to offer. It's my belief that we begin to accomplish that by working together for his benefit. I would just like to ask that you please consider yourself a part of this family, not because of Will but because you're Sam's mother and thereby, the most popular person at this gathering."

She smiled more brightly this time. "For the precious gift of having Sam with us this Christmas, you have my deepest thanks, along with my promise that I will do whatever I must to make being here, not only this holiday but any time you'd like, as comfortable as possible. Consider this your home, Zoe. I know you don't have family and maybe you don't need a mother, but if you'd let me be your friend, it would mean a lot to me." She released Zoe's hand. "Now, may I offer you a tissue or a hug, or both?"

Zoe wobbled a smile. "I'm sorry. You're wonderful, Maeve, and I'm not trying to be difficult, it's only that I'm—"

"Struggling, and the Branch family isn't helping," Maeve completed for her. Once again she opened her arms. "No strings attached, all right?"

"Thank you," Zoe said, moving into Maeve's embrace, letting the tears go at last. "I'll try, Maeve, I'll really try, I promise."

"Merry Christmas, Zoe," Maeve said, rocking her from side to side. "And thank you for the brag book. I cannot wait to show my friends. Two grandchildren in one year—I am a very rich woman."

Zoe laughed and hugged Maeve back, glad to be here despite all her worries, and even happier for Sam that he was with a grandmother who prized people, not possessions. "Sam is very lucky to have you, Maeve."

"Oh, honey," Maeve said, her own voice less than steady. "I'm the lucky one." She drew back then. "Don't give up on happiness, sweetheart. Less than a year ago, my life seemed unbearable, yet here I am with more love than in my wildest dreams. This is a tough time for you, but don't say no to love, wherever it comes from. It's the only thing that matters." She brushed Zoe's hair with one hand, and Zoe wanted to curl into that touch. "I know that you believe that, too, however difficult your road is just now. No one could have produced that beautiful child without love being the major ingredient."

"He's my world," Zoe said. "My miracle."

"He is that," Maeve agreed and held out a hand. "Ready to go back?"

Zoe wiped her eyes and nodded. "Will is blessed to have a mother like you."

"And don't think I don't remind him of that every so often." Maeve winked and drew her down the hall to join the celebration.

CHAPTER TWELVE

CHRISTMAS LED into New Year's, and though Will had invited Zoe out for an evening of celebration, they wound up celebrating at Maeve's house with Sam, Maeve, Chuck and Gerty while babysitting Sam's baby cousin Diane. Maeve had offered Penny and Craig a night on the town, their first since they'd become parents, and she'd made Zoe and Will the same offer, but Zoe had demurred and thankfully, Will hadn't pressed her. For her part, she'd compromised and not insisted on staying at home, just her and Sam.

The night might not have been glamorous or sexy, playing board games and having hilarious video game tournaments, letting Sam stay up until he fell asleep watching the ball drop in Times Square, but it felt safer to Zoe. As the close of Will's vacation approached, she was leery of getting physically involved with him again. Already, he was on daily calls to the shop in Kannapolis. Tomorrow Sam would return to school, and three days after that, Will would fly to North Carolina. Speedweeks in Daytona were a month away, but there was much for Will to do before then, several rounds of testing and various meetings with sponsors, among other things. He would be extremely busy.

If she could just hold out until she could get away from Will's overpowering presence—more importantly, get Sam over his dependence on seeing Will every single day—maybe life would resume some sense of normalcy. She would stop looking forward to seeing him herself.

She drew out the classified ads and opened them.

Just then, Sam entered the kitchen. "Dad and Uncle Bart will be here in a few minutes. Are you sure you don't want to come play paintball with us?" He glanced over her shoulder. "What's that for?"

She closed the paper hastily. Took a deep breath. "I need to find a job."

"What for?"

She smiled. "There's rent to pay and food to buy." She smoothed his hair. "And shoes for those feet that won't stop growing."

Sam grinned. "Dad says I might be even taller than him and Uncle Bart, as big as my feet are." Then a line formed between his brows. "Are we broke, Mom?"

"No, sweetheart." Though since she'd signed over Tanner's money to his parents, they'd be there soon if she didn't find some income, but that was her worry, not Sam's. "We're going to be just fine."

His eyes cast down. "I don't want Dad to leave. I wish we could go with him."

"He'll be very busy now. Nearly all his weekends will be taken up with racing until late this year, but he's going to fly here as often as he can on his days off."

"But I'll be in school. Can I skip?" Hope shone.

"Of course not. It'll be like it was before Christmas. He'll be waiting for you after school."

His face fell. "But I'll miss him. It won't be like now. I like seeing him every day."

"That's what happens with drivers, Sam. They've got busy schedules."

"That's not true," he protested. "Dad says he's gonna have time for me."

I wish he did, she thought, torn between wanting to protect him from reality and wishing she could somehow cushion the blow. "He loves you, Sam, it's not that. It's just that racing has a very long season, unlike other sports, and the commitment for a driver at your dad's level is huge." She pulled him in for hug, but he resisted. "You can talk to him on the phone every day. He already promised that." And she would kill him if he let Sam down.

"It's not enough," he shouted and drew back. "I could be with him all the time if you'd just let me. He said so. I could homeschool, and we could travel with him. You're the one who's making him go away!" He raced from the room, leaving Zoe reeling.

Just then, there was a knock on the door.

Zoe rose from her chair and contemplated ignoring what could only be Will. How dare he lobby her child against her? He knew nothing about raising a child, but here he was, taking advantage of Sam's longing for an extension of the never-ending vacation Will had created, when he knew good and well that he was the one letting Sam down. His life and his choices were the reason they were all in this fix.

She yanked the door open, and Will's wide grin faded. "What's wrong? Are you okay? Where's Sam?"

She started to slam the door in his face, but Will caught it—and her—before she could.

"What's going on, Zoe?"

She jabbed her finger in the direction of Sam's room, so angry she was speechless.

"Sam? Is he all right?" Will barged in and headed toward the hall.

Zoe caught his arm, only now realizing that Bart was present, too, but too furious to care. "He's blaming me because you told him he could be with you all the time if I wouldn't make you go away."

"Zoe." Will reached for her, and she slapped his hand away.

"Don't touch me."

Will's eyes were wide. "Calm down."

"Calm down? You sashay in here after spending God knows how much money giving Sam a holiday that's completely unrealistic, making him believe that every day with you would be like that if only his wicked witch of a mother wasn't so mean."

"I never said that, Zoe. You know me better than that."

"Do I? What I know is that you left me, and you'll do it to him, too—only he doesn't know that. He actually believes you when you say he comes first." Her voice had risen so loud that Sam came running.

"Mom? What's wrong? Dad!" Sam halted mid-stride, caught between worry and excitement.

"Hey, dude," Bart spoke for the first time. "Listen, your mom and dad need to visit for a minute. What say you and I go outside?" When Sam hesitated, he sweetened the pot. "I've got a handheld game you haven't seen yet."

The air was thick with fury and misery. She was ashamed to have lost control like this, to have Sam hear her screeching like a harpy. She wanted Will and Bart to both disappear—for good. Let her be while she came up with a plan to take care of her child.

Will yanked his gaze from hers, wiping the frown off his face and turning to kneel in front of Sam. "We'll be fine, son. I promise. You go with Uncle Bart, and I'll join you in a few minutes."

Sam looked between the two of them, still unconvinced. Zoe knew it was up to her. "Go on, sweetie. It's okay."

"Don't you hurt her," he said to Will in a voice that was a harbinger of the man he would become.

The quick glance Will shot at her was filled with blame. *Look what you've done to us,* it seemed to say.

Sam, she reminded herself. He was all that mattered. However furious with Will she was, she couldn't ruin this last day for her son. "He won't," she replied. Though he already had. "Go with Uncle Bart, and we'll be done in minute."

Done forever, maybe. All the doubts she'd had flooded back, making her wish she'd never told Will he had a child. There could be nothing for them but heartache—all of them. Not as long as Will was involved with the sport of stock car racing.

At last, Sam followed Bart out, if slowly. The door closed, and she was left with Will.

"What the hell just happened, Zoe?" Anger was there in his voice, yes, but also bewilderment.

"You tell me. He's devastated that you're leaving, just as I told you he would be."

"I never told him it was your fault."

"What did you tell him, then? Sam is not a liar."

He did a double take. "I didn't say he was. What's going on, Zoe? What's put this burr up your butt?"

"You don't get it, do you? You're so focused on your career, you're blind to everything else."

"Whoa! Slow down here. That's not fair, and you know it. I told you we could work it out, that you and Sam could come with me."

"And uproot ourselves from everything that's familiar, just to take a chance on you when—" *You left me before.*

"Are you ever going to let go of that, Zoe? Will you ever allow either of us to forget that I made a mistake? Anyway, how the hell do you think I'm going to support you and Sam if I stop driving? Even if I could quit, I'd be stuck in some dead-end minimum-wage job just like—" *You,* he didn't have to say.

"I never asked you to support me."

"Of course you didn't. I offered."

"No, you ordered me. Told me what my child deserves, what he needs—you, who's known him for a whole six weeks, when I've devoted my life to caring for him."

"Zoe, calm down."

"Calm down? You've turned my child against me, and I'm supposed to calm down?"

He shoved fingers into his hair and began to pace, his big frame taking up all the space in the room. Then he halted. Looked back at her. "You don't think it's tearing my guts out, knowing I have to leave him? You think that just because you've known him every second of his life that I can't love him like crazy, too? You're the one who won't give us a chance, Zoe. I want to give him everything. To provide for him—and for you, if you'd let me—but the only way I have to do that is through racing. The season is long, and I can't stand the thought that I'll only get to see him once a week and that only if I'm lucky." He returned to stand in front of her. "I don't know what to do. I don't set the schedule, and I don't control the sport. There's a lot I have to accomplish to succeed. Once it was enough just to show my old man, to show everyone who ever doubted wild Will Branch that I could amount to something." He clasped her shoulders, and his voice turned gentle. "But that's not enough anymore. What I want is to make my son proud, and to take good care of him—" Here his lips curved with rue. "And his mother, who's important to me all on her own."

When she kept herself rigid, he sighed and let her go. "How can I convince you to trust me, Zoe? What will it take to prove that I love my son? That I love—"

"Don't say it," she snapped. "Don't you dare say you love me, Will Branch."

"What if I do?" he asked softly.

She closed her eyes. Forced herself to resist how badly she'd wanted to hear those words years ago. She couldn't let herself be charmed by him. Seduced by him. The stakes were too high.

"All right," he said, disappointment heavy in his tone. "I won't say it because you so obviously don't welcome hearing it. But the fact remains that Sam wants to be with me, and I want to be with him. And you're standing in the way, Zoe, you and your distrust."

"Get out." She wheeled away, her chest tight and aching.

He exhaled a weary breath. "Please just give us a chance. Come to Daytona for as much of it as you can. We already know from Halesboro that Sam can keep up with his work, and Speedweeks are a spectacle he'll never forget."

"So you can keep wooing him with the glamour of his famous father's life, and our life here gets less and less bearable to him?"

"Zoe," he groaned. "This is not a competition. I'm trying to figure out a life for all of us, but you're so dead-set on fighting me that we're all going to lose in the end." He paused. "Why did you tell me about him if you had no intention of letting me be part of his life?"

"I didn't expect you to get this involved," she blurted.

His chuckle held more sorrow than amusement. "So is it possible that you might be wrong about me in other ways?" He approached her. Settled his hands on her shoulders. "I am not going to hurt him, sweetheart. I love him. I'm trying my best to figure this out. Won't you meet me halfway?"

Having him involved at all was more than halfway, in her mind. She sagged, all too aware that she might be unfair. "I'm so afraid, Will," she whispered.

"I know, honey." He slid his arms around her and bent his head to hers. "Please. Just give me a chance. Come to Daytona. Talk to the other moms on the circuit. Daytona's a zoo, I know, and it doesn't represent the normal routine for a driver, either, but—" He chuckled into her hair. "I just don't want to wait any longer to see either one of you. It's over a month away, and the time is going to be endless."

He turned her. "Don't you think I'm scared, too? Sam will love Daytona, but I already know you're set to hate it. If anything goes wrong, I risk losing you both, and that scares the living daylights out of me." Blue eyes held her gaze. "But I don't want to be a long-distance father, limited to phone calls and sporadic visits. I've missed so much of his life already."

He was laying his heart bare to her, and Zoe realized with a shock that she could hurt him, too. "I just don't see how it can work, but—" She shook her head. "All right. I'll talk to Sam's teacher, and we'll work something out for at least part of Daytona."

Will looked as vulnerable as she'd ever seen him. "Thank you." He brought her hand to his lips, clasped in both of his, and kissed her fingers. "I mean it, Zoe. Thank you." Then the cocky, arrogant Will Branch reemerged. "I'm going to show you it can work. I promise you it can. I'll make it happen." He started to give her a hug she wasn't at all convinced she welcomed, not when her doubts that this was the right choice were consuming her. She dodged, and they wound up in an awkward half dance, then finally separated.

"You'd better go," she said. "Sam and Bart are waiting."

"But I don't want to. Come with us?"

She shook her head. "I don't think so."

"Let me take you out to dinner after."

He was just too…there. Too big a presence already. He would take over all the space in her loneliness if she let him, and that would be a huge mistake. "I can't. It's a school night."

"Yeah." He sighed. "Can I at least kiss you?"

"Better not." She had to keep her wits, and Will's kisses blasted them to bits. "You all have fun."

"Come to the door with me, so he can see you're okay."

But I'm not. Nonetheless, she followed.

They waved at Sam, whose face relaxed in relief.

Will turned to her. "Thank you, Zoe. I mean it. I'm going to make this work."

She couldn't see how, but she kept her doubts to herself.

"I'll make arrangements to fly you in."

"I'll get our tickets myself."

Will laughed. "For Daytona this time of year? Honey, there's not a seat or a hotel room available for love or money."

She gulped. "You're not expecting us to stay with you." How would she ever keep herself apart? "You have to focus." It was the only argument that might prevail.

"I want you there. I'll do fine—better if I know where you are."

"Will, you'll go crazy with us underfoot for days. And anyway, what about your image? News of Sam is sure to get out, just with us being there, and for me to be in the same motor home…"

"Zoe." He reached for a lock of her hair. "Give it up. Kylie and Sandra are on the case, PR-wise, and I'm not hiding Sam from the world. I'm proud of him. Plus, if we're going to make this work, we have to try it for real. Anyway, I'm not kidding. People literally have reservations a year or more ahead." When she didn't relax, he sighed. "Look, if it gets bad, I'll bunk with Bart, okay?"

"But—" *Where will you be sleeping?* She wanted to ask. Mostly because she wasn't sure how she'd handle the temptation. Thank goodness Sam would be there to chaperone. "You need your rest. This is too important."

"Then—" he bent to her, pressing a quick kiss to her lips "—I suggest you stop arguing with me. It might hurt my concentration." His grin was unrepentant.

This was not the time to battle it out, not when Sam was hopping from one foot to the other in anticipation. She would call Kylie and see if there were other options.

"Go on. Your son is waiting."

"Can I tell him?" Then, in a moment of insight she'd never have expected from him, he shook his head. "Never mind. You should be the one. Otherwise, I'm being Fun Dad again, right?" At her nod, he smiled. "Surprised you, huh? I told you I'd show you, didn't I?"

"Go away." She practically shoved him out the door. "And yes—and thank you." She closed it in his face.

And listened to him laughing as he left.

CHAPTER THIRTEEN

"YOU ALREADY TALKED to that Haines guy from New York? The cop?" Zack Matheson asked Will in the garage at Daytona.

Will turned from where he was watching his team banging out a fender he'd damaged sliding into the fence and frowned at the driver parked next to him. "Yeah. You?"

"Not me, but he questioned my brother Chad."

Will had to lean closer to hear over the engines. "What about? Was Chad AWOL from the dinner like me?"

"No, because of the sabotage of Kent Grosso's car."

"Haines asked me about that, too. He's really focused on that wreck, isn't he? I forgot about the rumors that Chad was seen in the garage that night and might have been behind it."

"Chad sure wasn't happy about Kent wrecking our brother Trent and costing him two races that year, but he'd never stoop to messing with another team's car. No one ever found any evidence that he was responsible."

"Haines suggested that I could have killed Alan Cargill," Will said.

"What? Are you kidding?"

"Nope. He seemed more interested in Brent Sanford, though, especially once I could prove I was already gone."

"Those two sure hated each other, Brent and Cargill, after Cargill pointed the finger at Brent. He always held that Brent did it."

"Brent sure as hell lost a career over it. Can't imagine how that would feel."

"Will!" his crew chief yelled. "We need you."

"Duty calls," Will said to Zack.

"No problem. You ready for the exhibition race?"

"Can't wait." Will waved and left. He spent a few minutes conferring with Seth and the engine builder, but he kept checking his watch, glad that Texas was an hour behind the East Coast. He'd slip away first chance and make his daily call to Sam. It hadn't been easy to manage at times—he wasn't used to focusing on anything but racing while he was at the track. Working until the day was done, however late that went. Catching meals at odd hours.

Not exactly the type of schedule Zoe kept for Sam. He knew her doubts, understood that she was just waiting for him to screw up. Sometimes he resented her skepticism, her refusal to let the past go, to give him a break. A second chance.

But then he'd remember how good she was with Sam. How much he himself had depended on his mother's constancy when he was young—or grown, for that matter. Zoe was a very good—and protective—mother. Despite Tanner's treachery, she'd raised Will's son to be a terrific kid, and Will had to give her high marks for that—as well as for being strong enough to survive Tanner's mistreatment herself.

If he thought too much about what her life must have been like with Tanner, how Sam had grown up believing he wasn't worthy of a father's love, well, it was a good thing Tanner wasn't around, or Will would be tempted to do him bodily harm.

The final blame, though, went to Will himself. Yes, he'd been young and ambitious, crazy about racing, but if he'd stood up better to his father's bullying, Zoe and Sam could have had a very different life.

Only question was, if he were honest with himself: would that life have been better? Could Will have handled the constant tension between family and racing?

For that matter, could he do it now? Despite his claims to Zoe that they could make it work, he was a whole lot less than certain. He'd taken to watching the families in NASCAR, trying to understand how they managed.

"Will, we're ready. Saddle up!" Seth shouted.

Will glanced at his watch and swore. He'd lost a precious window of time to call Sam while woolgathering over an issue that was claiming too much of his attention, to the detriment of his racing. They didn't have much time left in the practice session, though, so he had no choice but to delay the call until after they'd shut down for the night. Track time was far from the end of what had to be done.

He would be cutting it close to Sam's bedtime, and Zoe would not be happy. He rubbed his forehead, weary of the struggle, and the season hadn't even started. He tried to forget Zoe's displeasure and focus on his child. Maybe there was no way, regardless of his wishes, to make the three of them work, but he knew one thing.

Sam would be delighted, no matter what time he called.

ZOE COULDN'T BELIEVE she'd agreed to be at Daytona for ten whole days. Sam had even done the dishes several times on his own, finished assignments that weren't due for weeks and kept his room spotless, just to show her that he was willing to do anything to be with his father.

She knew how he was missing Will, how each daily call—which, despite her misgivings, Will had never missed—absolutely made Sam's day. From her own brief conversations with Will, she knew the longing to be together was mutual.

So here they were, being picked up, by Sandra Taney instead of Mike, and driven to the track.

"I hope this isn't a terrible inconvenience," Zoe said.

"Not a bit," Sandra replied. "I was out getting supplies anyway. I'm having a bunko party tonight—girls only. We'd love to have you, if you're interested. Kylie will be there, along with some of the drivers' wives and girlfriends and some owners' wives, too—or in Patsy's case, an owner herself."

"Patsy Grosso?"

Sandra nodded. "You know her?"

"No, but Maeve wanted to introduce me to her." Zoe cast a sideways glance. "She, like her son, thinks I need to see that NASCAR families can work."

Sandra arched one eyebrow. "I've been wondering. Will's mind doesn't seem altogether on his racing these days, and it's not just Sam's name that comes up in conversation." She waited as though wanting Zoe to confirm that there was something between her and Will.

"It can't be me. I've made it clear that there's no future for us."

"Why not?"

Zoe glanced into the backseat, where Sam was ostensibly playing a handheld game Will had sent him—but she knew her son. "I'd rather not get into that right now."

Sandra saw where she was looking. "I hear you. Little pitchers. Instead, let me tell you a little about who's coming tonight. I especially need to explain something about Patsy's situation. I'm not betraying a confidence—someone else has made sure the news has traveled through the garage, however hurtful it might be."

"What do you mean?"

"It's a pretty amazing story—and a very difficult topic, even for someone as strong as Patsy. You'll love her, by the way. She's the gold standard for NASCAR wives and mothers—behind her guys all the way—at least until last year when she demanded that Dean stop racing, and they split up over it."

"Wow. That took guts. What happened to them?"

"He won the championship, and finally got his head out

of his behind and realized that nothing mattered more than Patsy. He retired, and they bought the team he'd driven for."

"Will isn't going to quit racing, so meeting her isn't likely to help me."

"I think it might, but regardless, what I need to alert you about is what's come to light recently, so you don't say something inadvertently. The upshot is that there's a mystery blogger saying that Dean and Patsy's daughter Gina is alive."

"Oh, my goodness. What happened to her?"

"That's the thing. No one ever knew there was a Gina. Turns out she was Kent's twin, but she was stolen at birth and died in the custody of her kidnappers, her body never found. At least, that's what Patsy and Dean have believed for the past three decades. It's tearing their hearts out to have to relive this. To wonder and hope but have no way to know for sure."

"How horrible." Zoe tried to imagine losing Sam as a baby. To lie awake at night and wonder if your child is hurting. "She must have been devastated, then and now."

"Patsy's tough, but this is really testing her. Both of them. They don't know what to do. What to believe." Sandra's look turned grim. "I'd like to get my hands on the coward who's using the Internet to hurt them without having the guts to come out into the open and explain why he or she thinks that baby didn't die. Can you imagine, after all this time, having to think about where your child might have been, what she might have suffered?" Sandra shook her head hard. "Anyway, that's why Patsy needs things like tonight. To be with friends and maybe escape a little." She glanced at Zoe. "NASCAR is a family, a tight-knit one. Maybe the families have to make sacrifices for a driver to succeed, but they're not alone while they're waiting for him. We're there for each other, all of us. And there are a lot of good times, too."

Her lesson was a pointed one, but Zoe forced herself not to be resentful that Will was enlisting help to stack the deck in his favor. "I'll have Sam tonight."

"No, you won't. His father and uncle have plans for him."

Zoe clenched her hands together in her lap. "Will hasn't discussed them with me."

"He will." Then Sandra reached over and patted her hand. "You're among friends, Zoe, if you'll let us be."

She was a nice woman, a kind one. Of course she didn't understand. She was a part of this world, and she was thrilled by racing. Zoe was neither. She took a deep breath and told herself to relax, however little she felt like doing it. "Thank you for the invitation," she said politely.

She didn't commit, however, to attend.

Will Branch had some explaining to do first.

"Look, Mom, it's the track!" Sam crowed from the backseat. "Only a few more minutes before we get to see Dad, right, Mrs. Taney?"

"Right you are," Sandra answered.

With a smile Zoe couldn't quite share.

WILL HAD FINALLY GOTTEN Sam to bed and was pretty proud of himself for remembering to make the boy take a shower and floss his teeth. At the same age, Will recalled, he and Bart had pulled every trick in the book to get out of both, though he had no idea why. Because girls weren't in the picture, probably, and hey, they were just going to get dirty again in the morning, so what was the big deal?

Heathens, the two of them had been, pure and simple. It was a miracle their mother had let them live.

Zoe was late. Really late. He'd tried her cell, but only gotten voice mail. She shouldn't be out at night walking alone.

Good grief. He was sounding like somebody's mother. This, along with the rest of the evening, gave him a new appreciation for what moms endured. Sitting and waiting, tending to the details of getting kids fed and bathed…how did they not go out of their ever-loving minds?

Okay. He slapped his palms on his thighs and stood up. Started to pace, then wheeled and made for the door. He had to do something. He had to make sure she was all right. He wouldn't go far, and he wouldn't leave Sam alone for long. Will locked the door and charged down the steps—

And nearly crashed into Zoe. He grabbed her shoulders to keep her from falling. "Where have you been?" he barked.

She glanced up at him with a goofy grin on her face. "Partying with the girls." She giggled. "Those girls do know how to party." She giggled again. "And you would be amazed at the gossip I heard."

"Are you drunk?" He studied her, then smiled. "You are."

"I am not." She drew herself up straight. "Patsy makes a really good margarita, but I only had…" She wrinkled her forehead. "I forget."

Will wanted to laugh. He'd never seen her like this, so loose and easy. He leaned back against the motor home and crossed his arms on his chest.

Zoe wobbled a little, so he quickly steadied her. "Whoa, there, Miss Sobriety. Let's go inside so you can sit down. Let me put you to bed."

Zoe slid against him, her moves sinuous…suggestive. "Why don't you come with me?" Her voice was husky as she fluttered those big gray eyes at him, her curves nestling into his body in a manner as old as time. "I think you should kiss me."

Why now? He wanted to groan at the unfairness. Zoe, warm and willing in his embrace…and drunk as a skunk. No way could he take advantage of her state, however much his body was demanding exactly that. He sought to distract her. "What gossip?"

"Hmm?" Her eyes were unfocused as she processed the question. "Um, Patsy said something about that man you mentioned. Alan Cargill?" She went silent for a long time.

"What about him?"

"He died. That's so sad…" She seemed in danger of drifting off again, but suddenly she refocused. "That detective found something on his BlackBerry that he thought might have to do with Dean."

"Dean Grosso? What?"

"I'm not sure." Her forehead wrinkled. "People were really interested, though." Then she brightened. "I know! He wanted Dean to explain a notation. Something like Ask D about G. Or was it Ask G about D?" She frowned up at him. "Patsy said Dean thought it might have something to do with a cereal company infterested in sponsoring Kent."

"GranolaPlus," Will supplied.

"I guess. Is that important?"

"Not to me," he said. "Just curious."

"But what really got to me was when Patsy mentioned the baby. People never knew about her?"

"Before my time." Will shrugged.

"That awful blogger. How can someone be so cruel? If the baby's alive, then that person should just come tell Patsy and Dean what they know." Her indignation faded, and her eyes filled with tears. "Losing a baby like that would kill me. Just kill me."

Good move, Slick. Get her maudlin.

She sniffed, then wiped her nose on the back of her hand. Will would have known she was intoxicated then if he hadn't before—fastidious Zoe would never use her hand. He wished he were the kind of guy who carried a handkerchief, but he offered her his shirttail, which was all he had.

"No, thanks. You need your shirt."

"If you'll come inside, I'll get you a tissue."

"I don't wanna come inside…unless you'll come with me." She snuggled into him. "Would you, pretty Will?"

"Pretty?" He didn't know whether to laugh or be insulted. "Guys aren't pretty."

"You are." She lifted her head and touched his hair. "All those beautiful curls…you should let them grow. And those blue eyes…such long eyelashes…"

Will glanced around to be sure no one in the known universe was listening. He would never live this down if any of his fellow drivers heard. "That will never happen. I keep it really short on purpose. And I am not pretty," he emphasized.

"I love your lips," she continued as if he'd never said a word. "Kiss me with them. They make me feel all melt-y."

"Melt-y?"

"Yeah." She sighed and rose to her toes, placing her mouth on his, starting out dreamy but quickly becoming pure fire in his arms.

Oh, sweet heaven, she was suddenly an octopus, her hands—surely more than two of them—roving over his chest, driving him out of his freaking mind while conspiring with her lips to shred his self-control. He wanted so badly to take her inside and make her his own.

His bed. Where Sam was this very minute. Asleep, he hoped to high heaven, but he couldn't be sure. "Zoe, stop."

"I don't want to," she protested. And started unbuttoning his shirt. "I want this gorgeous body. I want you—"

Will tore himself away from her before he completely lost all restraint.

When she started toward him, he held out a palm. "Don't touch me."

"Why?" She kept coming.

Oh, man, why couldn't she be this voracious when she was sober? He'd suspected that this appetite lay dormant inside her—she'd certainly responded very strongly their one night together at Christmas—but this was…amazing.

And damned unfair. He wanted to howl at the moon that she was here and she wanted him without reservation—

And he couldn't have her. She would never forgive him in the morning if he did.

"Zoe, honey, I'll take you inside." He spoke to her like someone soothing a wild animal whose bite was deadly. "Let's go inside, okay? It's getting cold out here."

She frowned. "I'm not cold." She fluttered her lashes. Pressed against him once more. "Are you cold, Will?"

"I am." Maybe this would work. "I need to go in."

"Poor Will. Pretty Will," she crooned.

Oh, good grief. This was a nightmare—on so many levels. Finally, he resorted to the only sure way to get her where he wanted her—well, not where he really wanted her, but where he needed her to go.

He bent his knees and swept her up in his arms.

"Ooh, how romantic!" she cried to the heavens.

And to every single person in the drivers' and owners' lot who might be listening.

"Shh, Zoe. People are sleeping."

"We could sleep," she said slyly. "Together. Wanna sleep with me, Will?"

He sighed. She had no idea.

"Let's sleep together." She flung out one arm. "It'll be so much fun!"

Will hushed her the only way he could—with his mouth.

And maneuvered her inside as fast as he could possibly manage.

CHAPTER FOURTEEN

ZOE WOKE IN BED ALONE and yelped when she opened her eyes and the bright Florida sunshine hit them. She sat up quickly—and just as quickly laid down, curling like a shrimp as her stomach rebelled.

Now she recognized her surroundings. Will's bed. In his motor home. She ventured a glance over her shoulder, but Sam was gone. "Sam?" she called out. "Will?"

She was sick, so sick. She must have come down with the flu. Then her gaze landed on the built-in bedside table. The glass of water, the bottle of aspirin with three already out. The note was propped up, which she had to squint to read.

It was Will's bold scrawl.

Morning, Sunshine.
Sam's with me at the garage. Stay in bed—you had a rough night. When we break for lunch, we'll come check on you.
Love, Will.

Love, Will. She tried to rise again, but her stomach was having none of it. *You had a rough night.*

Oh, no. Faint scraps of the night fluttered—margaritas, laughter. Patsy's tears.

Wishing she were with Will. That they could make this work.

Walking back to see him. Be with him.

Are you drunk?

She could feel him, that gorgeous body. See him grinning at her. Kissing her. She was unbuttoning—

Zoe, stop. Don't touch me.

She clapped one hand over her mouth. She was not going to remember this, not one more second. What she could recall was murky, but oh my word. Oh, no. Had she actually thrown herself at him?

She was very much afraid that she had. His laughing eyes stayed with her. Oh, mercy. What had they done? She glanced around the room wildly. Had they? With Sam right—

Suddenly, one more image hit her, Will wiping her mouth with a washcloth as she—

Oh, no. No, no, no. She'd been hanging over the toilet and Will—saw? Stayed with her?

This could not be happening. She had not made a total fool of herself in front of him. In front of all those women?

Zoe rose from the bed and nearly fell back into it. Sheer determination had her continuing across the room, walking into the bathroom.

When she saw her face in the mirror, she screamed. Matted hair, raccoon eyes, blotchy face—she whirled and buried her face in her hands. This was impossible. Unbearable.

What on earth exactly had she done?

You had a rough night. Her eyes went to slits as she imagined what she'd do to him if he told a soul.

It was beyond bearing. She couldn't stay here, couldn't possibly face anyone. She would pack, and she would find a ride to the airport where she would—

Will had sent Taney's plane for her and Sam. She had no money to buy last-minute tickets. Maybe Kylie would help her? No. God knows what she'd said or done at Sandra's. Maybe the woman was no longer speaking to her.

Pull it together, Zoe. She glanced out of the bathroom to the clock by Will's bed. Nearly noon. They might be here soon. Zoe bit her lip and marched toward the glass of water, the aspirin, every step a torture. She forced them into her raw stomach—sweet heaven, her abdomen was sore from throwing up. Then she grabbed clean underwear and refused to think of who had helped her change into the huge T-shirt that could only be Will's. She focused on one thing at a time—first, brushing her teeth, then a shower, hot as she could stand it.

When she was showered and dressed, brewing a cup of tea because the very notion of coffee had her stomach protesting, she paced the living area of the motor home.

And gnashed her teeth that once again, Will held all the cards. She'd let him drag her into his world again, had co-opted her son's loyalties. She resented that he so easily seized control and talked her into things she didn't want to be doing, using her child as leverage.

She had very little money and even fewer options. What should have been her home turf was Tanner's, a world where she didn't belong and couldn't stay.

Now she was trapped in another home turf where she didn't belong. Didn't want to. She'd heard those women last night, listened to their stories, and understood that they were close, as Sandra had claimed, and they were in some ways like sisters, united as women were when their men were in battle.

But Zoe didn't fit. She couldn't just hop on Will's coattails and be dependent again for every last thing. He would take care of her and Sam, she believed that—but she would, once more, be at a man's mercy, unable to support herself and her child if Will couldn't pull off what he'd promised and balance family and racing.

Didn't those women hear what they were saying? The slack was almost always taken up by the mothers. The sacrifice was enormous when the man you loved was crazy about racing and operating at the top level.

Will was one of them.

But she was not. He would never stop racing until he was forced out by age or, God forbid, injury. If she let things go further between her and Will, they would be subjected to the whims of Will's fortunes.

Zoe had not controlled her own destiny one single moment of her life until she'd filed for divorce from Tanner, and she'd learned very quickly how ill-equipped she was to take care of her child's future. With only a high school education and no job skills, that was not going to change until she did.

Will was right that Sam deserved better than what she could afford, but that didn't mean throwing herself at his mercy. It was right that Will contribute financially to Sam, but for herself she would propose a business arrangement. A straight-up loan to allow her to get the training she needed to support herself and her son without relying on Will. She would pay him back, every penny, with interest.

They would arrive at a schedule that would allow Will maximum time with Sam, even if it meant Sam flying to be at the track on weekends at times. She would be fair, and she would extend herself further than she wanted to from her comfort zone.

But only where Sam was concerned. She and Will would be co-parents, maybe even friends—but she would not give up her life again. She just wasn't like those women she'd met last night, however admirable she found them. They were taking too big a risk with themselves and their children.

More settled, Zoe made her way to the kitchen to make herself some toast and see if her stomach would cooperate.

Just then, the door opened, and Will stepped inside.

ZOE WHIRLED and clutched her chest.

"Hey, there." He found himself grinning at first, relieved

to see that puking up her toenails hadn't killed her and impressed that even a night that rough hadn't dimmed her beauty one bit. He even thought he preferred her this way, barefoot and her face free of makeup. "How are you feeling?"

"Where's Sam?"

He lifted his eyebrows, only now sensing the chill in the air. "With Ryan, playing soccer."

"Where?"

"He's fine, Zoe. Kylie's with them. I didn't stay because I was worried about you." Not a trace of the warm, willing woman of last night remained. He'd been right. She wouldn't have forgiven him for taking advantage of her ardor. He was a little surprised, though, that she couldn't even stoop to saying thank you for his own lost night's sleep as he cared for her. "You're welcome."

"What?"

His own temper, never far from hand, stirred. He'd had a hell of a morning already. The car was a disaster, a laundry list of things wrong with it, and having to keep up with Sam was a distraction he didn't need. Everyone on the team was edgy—the stakes were enormous for this season, and they seemed to be going backward with the car. Seth had been snapping at him all morning, and Will's mind had kept drifting to Zoe, hoping she was all right. Smiling foolishly at memories of her at inopportune moments. "Maybe I should just go."

"Maybe you should."

"Damn it, what's wrong with you? I'm not the one who drank too much. I'm the one who held your hair over the toilet. I know you're probably embarrassed about how you threw yourself at me last night, but you don't have to be. Drinking too much does that, but I'm not complaining. I wasn't even going to mention it."

"Then don't. I want to leave. I want to go home."

If that didn't just— "Go ahead. But you leave Sam here. He's having a great time."

Her eyes popped. "I can't…Sam can't…" She frowned fiercely. "Sam goes where I go."

"He's my son, too. I say he stays here. You don't want to fight me on this, Zoe."

She looked as if he'd slapped her. "You'd do that?" she asked dully. "Behave like Tanner? Use your money to trap me?"

"What? No. God, no. That's not—"

Just then, a cell phone rang. Will reached to answer, then realized his was silent. "I think that's yours."

"What?"

"Your phone."

Like a sleepwalker, she picked it up, opened it and listened, her face perplexed—until it went sheet-white. Zoe sagged back against the bar. "No. It can't—" She glanced up at Will with fear in her eyes.

He crossed the space in seconds. "What's wrong?"

She shook her head at him, then glanced down, concentrating hard. "You think what you want, Louise." She looked like a cornered animal. "You don't know what Tanner—"

Will reached for the phone, but she turned away. "That's not—" Her shoulders sagged, and she flipped the phone closed.

"Talk to me, Zoe. Let me help."

Slowly she turned to him, her face stricken. "I'm sorry, Will."

"For what? We had a fight. We'll have more, I'm sure, but—"

She held up a hand. "We need to find Kylie. And Sam. Oh, God, Sam. I have to get to him." She started toward the door in a panic.

He snagged her arm. "Tell me what happened."

She shook him off, frantic now. "I have to get Sam first before—"

"All right, all right. Calm down, Zoe. Tell me what this is about."

At the doorway, she halted. "Will. This is…it's bad. I'm so sorry you're being dragged into it."

"Into what?"

"Tanner. The toxicology's back. It was definitely suicide, and—" She pressed trembling lips together. Drew a deep breath. "There's a story on the Dallas news that it was a love triangle gone bad. That you and I duped him, his best friend and his wife cheated on him and had a love child who was passed off as his. That—" She gripped his arm. "That, after all, you're the son of Hilton Branch, embezzler and adulterer. They're…they're dragging your whole family into the scandal."

Will stared at her. "But it's not true. We didn't—" He shut his mouth as quickly as it had opened. Didn't he, of all people, know that the public appetite for gossip was endless, that the truth was only one of its victims? "Hell. Here we go again. And my new sponsor—" He grasped Zoe's waist and pulled her along to match his long stride as he whipped out his phone and punched in Kylie's speed-dial number. "We've got a problem," he said when she answered. "A big one. Are you still with Sam and Ryan?" At her affirmative response, he went on to explain what had happened as concisely as possible.

He had to give Kylie credit. She could think fast. "Yeah, I agree. We're almost there now. I can see the boys. Let us round them up, and you grab Sandra and Taney. We'll meet at my motor home. That way the boys can play video games while we plan." At her agreement, he disconnected.

"Will," Zoe said a little breathlessly. "I'm really sorry for whatever trouble this is going to cause you, I honestly am. About what I said before—"

He halted and glanced down. "That's not a discussion we have time for right now. I'm due on the track in just over an hour, and there's a lot to do before then." He bent to her.

"Maybe I deserve some of what you said, but not all of it, not by a long shot, but get this one thing straight. Not once have I tried to do anything but what I hoped was right for you and Sam. Maybe I screwed up somehow—I probably did—but you don't just walk away from me, and you damn sure don't take Sam away from me for spite."

"There's no spite involved. How dare you—"

"Hey, Dad! Did you see my goal?" Sam called.

He yanked his attention from her. "Sure did, son. Hey, grab Ryan. It's time for lunch. We're meeting his mom at our place." With effort, Will kept all the fury out of his voice.

"Okay!"

Will looked back at Zoe, grinding his jaw. "Damn it, Zoe. I'm under pressure everywhere I look, and I'm trying my best. Would you please just lighten up and trust me a little? Is it so much to ask?"

If anything, she stiffened more. "Pressuring you was never my intention. Just the opposite, in fact. I have no interest in being a burden to you."

Her tone was so tight, he wanted to shake his fists at the heavens and howl because they'd gotten so far off track and he had no idea how it had happened.

Will forced himself to take one deep breath, then another, and grab hold of his blasted temper before things got any worse. As the boys raced toward them, he was conscious of time evaporating. "Please, Zoe. Can we talk about this tonight after the exhibition race? Please?"

"Hey, Mom? You feeling better now? Did you see my goal?"

Zoe cast an apologetic glance at him, then turned to Sam. "Yes, and yes." Her voice, though strained, brightened. "How do hot dogs sound, guys?"

At their cheers, she turned and headed back the way they'd come.

Leaving Will to shake his head.

And wonder what could happen next.

CHAPTER FIFTEEN

UNFORTUNATELY, finding out didn't take long.

While the boys were inside playing games, swilling down juice and stuffing themselves with the hot dogs that were making Zoe's stomach roll, Kylie and Sandra had honed the party line. Had started making calls to get their message in first before the rumors from Dallas began swirling.

Will's sponsor was not happy. The Lundgren Group needed the public confidence as it tried to extend its market share. There should be no whiff of anything shady, and Will's life just kept providing scandal. Embezzling was bad, a mistress was not good…they'd gone along with the illegitimate son after much discussion—but suicide? A love triangle gone bad?

If McKay Lundgren wasn't happy, Will's team owner wasn't happy. And NASCAR expected its drivers to be squeaky-clean.

Zoe could see the strain on Will. She'd tried to convince the group that it would be best for her and Sam to leave and let the story die down.

Will was having none of it. Kylie understood the urge to protect her child, Zoe could see, but she agreed with Will. Sandra, though, was less certain, but Will had dug in his heels.

"I'm not apologizing for Sam or you. I'm not ashamed of you, and that's what people would think. You have to face these people down, Zoe. I know from experience."

So here they were, walking toward the gate of the drivers' lot on their way to the hauler. The exhibition race was in just over two hours, and Zoe was worried sick for Will. However angry she'd been earlier, all that had vanished as she'd watched the toll on him.

And then she saw them. A crowd of reporters just past security.

"Your dad had a mistress, so you wanted one, too, Will? Is this a family tradition?"

"No comment," Will said as they'd agreed, and kept walking, one arm around Zoe and the other around Sam.

"What about you, Ms. Hitchens? How do you feel, knowing you drove your husband to suicide?"

"Are you ashamed of what you did, Will? Why didn't you claim your son until now?"

"Leave my dad and mom alone!" Sam shouted.

The microphones and cameras zoomed toward him, and Zoe felt cornered. They shouldn't have come.

Will interposed his body between the reporters and them. "My rep has a statement for you. Leave my family alone."

"How can you concentrate on driving tonight, Will?"

"The same way I did all last year when you vultures wouldn't leave me and my brother alone. Now get the hell away from my family." He took a menacing step forward.

Though the reporters stepped back, their questions didn't stop. "What does Taney have to say about this? How are you going to keep your new sponsor? Think you'll lose your ride?"

Zoe watched Will absorb each question like a blow but remain standing. She was sick at heart to be costing him this way, especially knowing that he had to go on the track very soon and needed every bit of his focus.

Then reinforcements arrived. "Come with me, Zoe," Bart said, scooping up Sam.

"But... I can't leave Will."

"Kylie's right behind me with Sandra and Taney. He'll be okay."

"He won't—" She turned on Bart furiously, then saw the fear in Sam's eyes.

"We have to help him, Mom. Let me down, Uncle Bart." Sam started wriggling to be released.

Bart only tightened his grip and grabbed Zoe, too, towing them both along until they were out of sight of the melee. "Listen to me," he said firmly, lifting Sam's chin. "Your dad loves you, and that's what dads do—they protect their families. He can take care of himself, I promise. You've heard a little about what our father did last year, I know." He waited for Sam's nod. "We've both had to deal with a lot of hard questions. We handled it, and we still went out on the track and kicked butt. Your dad will do that tonight."

Sam looked at her. "Did my...why did Tanner kill himself? Was it my fault?"

She and Will had tried to explain back in the motor home, but a nine-year-old should never have to know that suicide existed. One more black mark on Tanner's record, that he'd put them all in this situation. Frantically, she sought for an explanation that Sam could understand. "Tanner was a very unhappy person, honey, but he was that way long before you or I met him."

"She's right, Sam," Bart said. "Will and I knew him from when we were younger than you. He was unhappy, and he made the wrong choices. He lied to your parents, and he wasn't a good dad to you."

Sam's forehead wrinkled. "I don't understand how he could do it."

"None of us do, honey. I wish so much that you'd never had to know about any of this, but we're here for you, all of us. We love you—your dad and Uncle Bart, and Grandma Maeve and Grandpa Chuck."

Bart crouched beside where she'd taken Sam into her

arms. "You're a Branch now, Sam, and we Branches stick together. Tough times or great times, we don't give up on each other."

"I want my dad," Sam said brokenly. "I want them to leave him alone." He lifted his head and looked at Bart. "What if he wrecks because they've upset him?"

Zoe's heart clenched because she was terrified of the same thing.

"Not gonna happen," Bart said with perfect confidence in his tone. "Your dad's tough. We Branch men are tough." He clasped Sam's shoulder. "He's a professional—nearly as good as me." Bart managed a grin, though Zoe could see the worry in his eyes.

"Uh-uh, Uncle Bart—" Sam shrugged, a faint trace of mischief stirring. "I'd say he's got the advantage."

Bart slapped a hand over his heart. "You're killing me, dude. I thought we were clear on this. I mean, Will's good and all, but, hey…this is your Uncle Bart we're talking about. You'll be just as happy standing in Victory Lane with me, right?"

Sam's head shook fervently. "Sorry, Uncle Bart. I love you and all that, but I gotta root for my dad. You can come in second, though."

"Thanks, champ." He tousled Sam's hair. "You're all heart."

When Sam looked a little worried, Bart chucked him on the chin and leaned closer. "I'm not gonna let him win on Sunday, but it's okay with me if he wins the exhibition race," he whispered loudly.

Sam recovered enough to snort. "My dad will win both. I don't mind if you win your qualifying race, though, since you're not in the same one."

"You're all heart, my man." Bart sighed. "Guess I'm gonna have to get my own son if I want somebody rooting only for me, huh?"

"You're really a good driver, though, Uncle Bart," Sam replied earnestly, the conflict evident on his features. "If I wasn't cheering for Dad to win, I'd definitely pick you."

"I know you would, sport." He gave Sam a quick hug. "And you're right to be for your dad first. He wants to make you proud of him 'cause he's so proud of you." He rose and held out a hand to each of them. "Now let's get you to your dad's hauler. If he and I don't make the drivers' meeting in time, we're both in trouble."

"Can we wait for Dad?"

Just then, Sandra caught up to them. "He's already on his way. He just took a different route."

"But we'll see him, right? Before he races?"

Zoe had the same question. She felt a piercing need to reassure herself that Will really wasn't unnerved by what had happened, would be able to focus on his driving and not be distracted.

"Absolutely," Sandra said. "You go on, Bart. I'll escort them over."

"Thanks, Sandra. Bye, sport, Zoe. See you in Victory Lane." Bart winked at Sam.

"Good luck, Uncle Bart," Sam called out after him.

Zoe ran to catch up with him. "Thank you, Bart. I didn't know what to say."

"No problem. I'm sorry it happened to you."

She worried at her lip. "Will he really be okay out there?"

"He will," Bart said. "He has to. He needs to win badly—never more than now."

"I've just made things so much harder for him."

"You didn't do anything, Zoe. You're not responsible for Tanner's actions, either. Will's had worse to deal with."

She knew that Bart was only being kind. The stakes for Will had just ratcheted.

But Bart had to concentrate, as well, so she didn't argue. "Good luck, Bart. Drive safely."

He flashed her a grin. "You can come kiss me in Victory Lane, you know."

"And fight off all your conquests?" The Branch brothers attracted women in droves, she'd witnessed many times already since she'd arrived. "Thanks, but I'm not trained in martial arts. And anyway," she said, grinning back, "Sam's right. Will's going to win."

"I get no respect." He rolled his eyes.

She lifted to her toes and kissed his cheek. "Be careful, Bart. And thank you again."

He waved and took off at a jog.

WHEN WILL FINALLY arrived at the hauler, he had only moments to spare. He'd had about enough of people for the moment—everyone either wanted to give him crap or lecture him or dig for details.

He just wanted to get in his car and forget the world.

"Dad!" Then sixty pounds of boy landed in his arms. Sam squeezed him hard and spoke low. "I told Uncle Bart he couldn't win because you're going to. I know you will, Dad." Then his voice dropped even lower. "I'm sorry that all those people want to ask questions about me."

Will's world narrowed to one worried pair of blue eyes. He held on to Sam but crouched to bring them face-to-face. "Those people don't bother me, unless they hurt you. Did they?"

Sam lifted one shoulder. "Nah. Branches are tough, Uncle Bart said. That's right, Dad, isn't it? And I'm a real Branch even if my last name is Hitchens?"

Will's shoulders sagged. One more detail to add to what he was juggling. "Of course you are," was what he said, though. And smiled. "The best one, if you ask me."

Sam's little chest puffed out. "Nuh-uh. You are, Dad. And I know you're gonna win tonight. Sunday, too." He grinned. "I told Uncle Bart so."

"Bet he didn't think much of that."

Sam leaned closer. "I told him he could come in second, though."

Will chuckled. "Nice of you." Kylie caught his eye and tapped her watch. "Sorry, son. I have to go." He'd give a lot to take Sam with him for driver introductions, but things were too touchy with both his sponsor and Taney just now.

"Go get 'em, Dad." Sam hugged him once more, and Will returned it.

Then he rose. Saw Zoe standing there, looking worried. "It's going to be okay," he told her. But he could see that she didn't believe him. He crossed to her. "A kiss for luck?"

"I haven't brought you much of that lately."

"Hush." He caught her chin, restricted himself to one soft kiss when he wanted much more. "I wish you could both walk me to the car, but…"

Her eyes darkened. "I understand. Not the best time." She slipped her arms around his waist. "Be careful, Will." She stepped back immediately, her lovely face lined with sorrow and regret.

"See you in Victory Lane, babe." And laid one more kiss on that sweet, sultry mouth. Ruffled his son's hair, then left quickly.

And tried to wipe everything but the track from his mind.

He wanted to make Sam proud. Zoe, too. More than he'd wanted anything in a very long time.

BUT THE RACE turned out to be a disaster for Will, and Zoe was sick about it. Sam was very disappointed, but he was more concerned about his dad.

Out of a field of twenty-four for the exhibition race, Will finished twenty-fourth. Listening to him on the scanner and watching the race from inside the hauler, Zoe could tell both from Will's conversations with Seth and the expressions of the people around her that hardly anything had gone right all night.

Some of them were blaming Will for being distracted. Will was furious over the car's handling. Others blamed the tires they'd been given. The bad luck of being spun in Turn Four by an idiot.

Whatever the cause, Will's first race of the year—the one for which he'd had such high hopes, due to both the size of the purse and his team's need to establish momentum after the upheaval last year—did not bode well for the rest of the season.

Zoe felt, more than ever, that they didn't belong here, she and Sam. That they were part of the problem, a big part.

And when Will arrived at the hauler, she was absolutely sure.

"It's okay, Dad," Sam said. "It's not your fault."

Flanked by a very unhappy sponsor's rep and an angry crew chief, sweaty and so exhausted the bones on his face stood out like a death mask, Will glanced at his son, opened his mouth, then shook his head and walked away.

"Dad?" Sam tried to catch up with Will. "It wasn't your fault—"

"Not now, Sam," Will interrupted. "I can't... Go see your mother." He stepped around his child, then disappeared into the conference room at the back.

"Mom?" His little face stricken, Sam had tears in his eyes.

I knew it. I knew this would happen. Damn you, Will Branch. But being right didn't make Zoe feel one iota better, nor did the pitying glances of the team. The atmosphere was thick and poisonous. "Come on, sweetheart. It's been a hard day. Let's give your dad time to relax a little, okay? Want to go see what Ryan's doing?"

"I want to wait for Dad." Completely out of character for him, Sam was nearly whining.

"Come on, Sam." If she didn't get out of here, she'd scream. "Now."

Her heart aching, her own temper stirring, Zoe left with Sam in tow.

They would definitely pack and go.

But she would give Will Branch a piece of her mind first.

FINALLY SAM WAS ASLEEP, inconsolable that Will had never shown up. Zoe had tried to sleep herself, but she was both furious and heartsick. She was pacing the living area in the darkness, wishing she'd insisted on departing tonight.

But Sam had pleaded. Though Will had hurt him by turning away, Sam still gave him the benefit of the doubt. Instead of Zoe soothing him over his father's mistreatment, it was Sam who'd rallied to be the voice of reason. *It's okay, Mom. I know he didn't mean it. He was just really tired.* Her child's capacity for forgiveness seemed endless, yet she saw the desperation in his eyes, the need to believe that yet another father figure didn't find him unworthy of his attention.

That was what had Zoe walking the floors, cursing Will Branch nearly as much as she despised herself for creating this situation. If she'd never told Will about Sam, her child would not be lying one room away with tearstains on his cheek.

The door opened, and Will stepped inside.

Instead of flipping on the light by the entrance, he only stood there for a moment, outlined by the full moon shining through the skylight.

His shoulders, usually so broad and filled with the energy he emitted in waves, were bowed in defeat. He sagged against the wall, head down.

Zoe felt like an intruder, witnessing this very private moment. She began to edge backward, as though she could somehow escape his notice.

His head rose swiftly. "Zoe?"

She froze. No idea how to respond.

"Can't sleep?" he asked. In the dim glow, she saw his head shake wearily. "I'd like to sleep for a thousand years or so. Listen—" He approached slowly. "I'm sorry I didn't get back in time to talk to Sam."

"I knew you'd hurt him. I knew it." All sympathy fled. Anger replaced it.

"I'm sorry. I never meant to. I just couldn't handle pity on top of everything else."

"You have to handle whatever you're handed when it's your child."

"Well, excuse me for being human. It's been a hell of a day."

"I told you we had no business coming here."

He whirled away, threw his hands up. "Of course you did." He wheeled back. "Because you're the perfect parent, right, and I'm incompetent. Doesn't matter that you've had nearly ten years of practice and I've had a few weeks. I've been tried by judge and jury and sentenced to hang for one mistake." He approached. "One freaking mistake, Zoe."

"Keep your voice down. He hasn't been asleep long. He was too busy making excuses for you because he's so desperate for you to love him."

Will halted in mid-stride. Even by moonlight, she could see his devastation.

He retreated. Collapsed on the couch. Raked fingers through his hair and let his head fall back. "I do love him. He's got my goddamn heart in that small fist. I don't know how to say enough that I'm sorry. It's just that everyone's on my back."

"We'll be gone in the morning, so you won't have us to deal with."

His head whipped toward her. "Don't. Please, Zoe. I screwed up, all right? But don't punish me like this. Don't take my boy away. It won't happen again, I swear." He leaned forward. "I'm trying. I'm doing the best I can. Hell, in past years, I'd have been punching someone's lights out or wrecking this place. You have no idea how hard I've been choking down my temper." He rose again, walked to her. "What do I have to do, get on my knees and beg? I will. I'll do whatever it takes. Don't part Sam and me on a bad note like this. Give me a second chance. Please."

Will was a proud man, and she'd only been a witness to the pressures he'd been under, not trapped in the middle of the pressure cooker as he was. For all her fears for her child, Zoe found her anger leaking away as this man—who'd already been pummeled by the press, the crowd, the team and what she realized now had to be humiliation at letting down his son—offered up whatever was left of his pride to her.

Her concerns that she and Sam were a negative influence on his racing hadn't diminished—if anything, they'd grown stronger—but she couldn't hold on to her fury. He was right. She'd been at this a long time, parenthood, and he was trying his best.

"You don't have to beg." She had to swallow hard to be able to finish. "I'm sorry, too, Will." She placed her palm on his cheek. "This has been a really rough day for you. I just…it felt too much like Tanner, turning away from him, and I…"

He leaned into her hand and closed his eyes. "I understand. I got out of the meeting with whatever hide was left after they peeled it off me, and I wanted to apologize to him—and you—but you were gone. I went to Bart's and showered so I wouldn't wake anyone, and I probably should have slept there, but I just…" He hesitated. "I wanted to be with you. Both of you. I didn't know if you'd still be here."

She smiled faintly. "Don't think I wasn't tempted."

"I'm sorry. Really. If I'd stopped to talk to him, I was afraid I'd lose it." His smile was rueful. "I didn't think breaking down and bawling would do much for my sponsor's opinion of me. That little face and the love and the fact that he, a little guy who's had it so rough, wanted to console me—" His voice cracked.

Zoe saw that the strain hadn't left him, that he was not only exhausted but weary to his soul, and she couldn't withhold herself from him. She rose to her toes and wrapped her arms around his neck. Gathered him in.

Will lowered his head to her shoulders, and she felt him surrender to what she was offering, his arms gripping her so tightly she could barely breathe.

But she didn't care. She held on. He was a good man. He was nothing like Tanner. The issue of whether she and Sam aided or hurt his cause was still to be resolved, but—

Not tonight. He'd had enough, this weary warrior. He needed rest and soothing. "Take the bed tonight," she offered. "I'll make a pallet for Sam. You need your rest."

"It's not the bed I need, it's you. I need you, Zoe," he said into her neck, and the warmth of his breath made her shiver.

I need you. Will had never said that to her before. *I want you,* yes. But never need. For this proud man, the admission was tantamount to a declaration of—

No. Not love. She couldn't think about loving Will Branch, not now. She could feel the possibility of it within her, how the shining gleam of it had already stolen into her heart like a cat burglar.

But that was not for tonight. The day had been long and difficult for both of them, but Will had borne the brunt of it.

Tonight was for comfort. For refuge.

He straightened but didn't let go, lifting her off her feet. His mouth cruised up her neck, but when she froze, he halted. Set her down.

It was up to her, was the message. Even now, as badly as he needed her, wanted her, he wouldn't force her.

She smiled up at him and pressed her mouth to his even as she cradled his head in her hands. Began to massage his skull, then moved down to neck and shoulder muscles tight with tension.

Even as he kissed her deeply, hungrily, he groaned a little.

"Lie down," she said.

"I thought you'd never ask." From somewhere he mustered a wicked grin.

"I'm going to give you a massage. You're tied up in knots."

He blinked. "But… I thought you…" He shook his head. "Uh-uh. You were getting melt-y, I could feel it. I'm not giving up my chance at getting you in bed."

"Who said you were?" She grinned. "And why do you say melt— Oh, no!" She slapped one hand over her mouth. "Did I say that out loud? The other night?"

His smile widened. "What happens if I say yes?"

She closed her eyes. "You won't. I'm not going to listen. Now—" She opened the sheet he'd folded on the sofa and spread it on the floor. "Lie down. Take off your shirt."

"Wanna help me?" Another devil's grin.

She decided to surprise him. "Yes." She slicked his T-shirt up his belly, then over his head.

"Whoa, baby." He waggled his eyebrows. "Jeans, too?"

He was recovering his innate sense of mischief, but she hadn't forgotten the discouragement she'd seen. "Will." She pressed a kiss to his mouth. "Just relax. Let me take care of you for a change."

All humor fled. "I don't know how."

He was always in charge, she realized. Despite his devil-may-care image, Will was the one who took care of other people, not the reverse. "Start by lying down on your stomach. Let go, Will, just for tonight. Okay?"

He studied her for long moments, then grasped her hand and brought it to his lips. "Okay. I'll try."

"Good. I'll get some lotion and be back in a minute."

When she returned, he had complied, stretching out on

the sheet. Lacking a massage table, she did her best, beginning with long strokes down the length of his back as she knelt over him, trying to ignore the sheer male beauty of him. Resolutely she focused on working the tension out of his body, bit by bit. At first he insisted on talking, teasing, but she could tell her efforts were working when he first went quiet.

Then went to sleep.

Zoe kept on for a while longer, working her way over his neck, his shoulders, down his muscled arms and even into his fingers, guessing that driving would strain all of them, even if he hadn't had tons of other pressures on him this day.

It felt like a ministry of sorts, a soothing of Will's soul and not only his body, a way to get inside his defenses and tell the deepest part of him that she was there for him, that she cared.

Probably too much.

At last, when her own arms were shaking from the exertion, Zoe stopped and settled beside him, watching a face that had been precious to her so long ago…but was becoming even more so now. It didn't stop her from having misgivings.

But she'd follow her own advice and let go for the night. Let tomorrow take care of tomorrow.

When she began to rise to make up the sofa for him and seek her own bed, he stirred a little and frowned. "Zoe?" One hand opened, reaching for her, and she told herself it was to keep him from waking and destroying her work and had nothing to do with her own wishes.

But whatever the reason, she laid down beside him and pressed her palm to his back, much as she had with Sam when he was little and restless.

Will sighed and relaxed, and the strain once again eased from his face. His dear and handsome face.

Zoe smoothed his hair and pressed a kiss to his shoulder.

Then she curled up against him.

And settled in to watch over his sleep.

CHAPTER SIXTEEN

"Pssst! Dad!"

Will jolted at the sound of Sam's voice. For a minute, he couldn't figure out exactly where he was.

Then Zoe sighed and shifted against his side. His body's immediate response to her nearness had him wondering exactly how a dad was supposed to deal with a child's presence when said dad couldn't think about anything but the child's gorgeous mother.

He settled for removing his arm from Zoe and pressing one finger to his lips for silence.

Sam grinned and nodded.

Carefully, Will got to his knees, then bent and lifted her in his arms.

Zoe sighed and nestled closer. "Will…"

Hoo, boy. He cast a quick glance at Sam, whose grin had spread so wide his face might split. Will didn't know what else to do but wink.

Even stiff from sleeping on the floor, he hadn't felt this great in a long time…well, except for that one amazing Christmas morning after he and Zoe had made love.

Still, he thought as he laid her in the bed and covered her, pausing to place a tender kiss on her forehead, he hadn't expected to wake up with such hope after one of the worst days of his life. He'd approached the motor home as though stepping up to the gallows, knowing how badly he'd screwed up.

But he'd fallen asleep with Zoe's hands on him and awakened with her at his side, warm and cuddly, and his child's face was wreathed in smiles.

How did a day start out any better?

Filled with hope, Will closed the bedroom door quietly, made a stop in the bathroom, then returned to his son.

Smiling or not, Sam deserved an apology. "I'm sorry, son. About last night—"

Sam shrugged it off. "Forget it, Dad. You were really tired, and you were discouraged. I know how it feels to try really hard and not succeed."

The reminder that Tanner had frequently expressed to Sam that he didn't measure up, even when Sam tried his best at sports he wasn't good at or interested in, made Will furious at Tanner all over again.

But this was not the time to focus on Tanner. "Regardless, I should have done better with you. No matter how many people were waiting to chew on my butt, it was wrong of me. I appreciated that you wanted to make me feel better, I—"

"It doesn't really help when you're disappointed in yourself, does it?"

"How'd you get to be such a wise old owl?"

Sam's eyes widened, and he giggled. "You're funny, Dad." He was sunny again, and Will wondered how he'd ever deserved such a blessing in his life.

"Funny, huh? Speaking of which, since your mom won't know, want to see if there are any cartoons on right now?"

"Don't you have to qualify today?"

"I do, and I have about a zillion people to meet with beforehand, but—" he held up his palms "—not for a little while. Let's eat some bad cereal and watch cartoons, okay?"

"Yeah!" Sam jumped into the air, then hugged him.

"Shh. If your mom wakes up, we're toast, you know."

Sam's eyes danced. "Right. Sorry."

"Keep the volume down, and I'll get the bowls." With a spring in his step, Will began the morning.

With fresh hope.

LESS THAN TWENTY-FOUR HOURS after the hauler had been a cave filled with gloom, cheers rang out, and Zoe was glad she'd relented and come here to watch qualifying. Thanks to Kylie's press release, reporters had moved on to the next story.

Will had invited her and Sam to come to their pit box and watch, but Zoe was terrified that somehow she was bad luck. She'd even worn the locket he'd given her, hoping it would counteract any bad influence she might be. However much he'd argued and cajoled, she'd still been afraid that being on top of the hauler was still too close. The view, though, was amazing and Sam was beside himself, even before Will qualified first.

"He did it, Mom! He got the pole! My dad is on the pole for the season's biggest race!" Sam was leaping and dancing, slapping high fives with the team. "My dad's the best, isn't he?"

"He sure is, kiddo," said Taney.

"You bet he is," crowed Kylie. "Want to go see him now? Zoe? Come with me to meet him for the photos?"

"I don't—" Yes, she wanted to, but—

"Come on, Mom. Dad will want us there. It's a really big deal, you know."

In the end, she conceded and followed Kylie, threading through the garage area while Sam held her hand, skipping and calling out to every person he knew—a surprising number, in fact. "My dad got the pole! Did you know my dad got the pole?"

He spotted Bart crossing the asphalt. Bart hadn't done well enough to grab the second spot on the front row, but in a normal race, Sam had explained to her, he'd have been well up front, occupying the third row. Due, however, to the unique system of setting the field for Daytona, all the drivers would race on Thursday night in one of the two qualifying races, and the finishes there would determine the rest of the field.

Bart would have another chance to be near the front, it appeared.

But Will, however he finished in his qualifying race, would not lose the pole.

"Uncle Bart, my dad got the pole!" Sam launched himself at Bart, chattering a mile a minute.

Zoe felt sorry for Bart, who was no doubt disappointed. He was every bit as competitive as his twin. He, however, had no new scandal attached to him. No sponsor ready to bolt. And he'd finished fifth in the exhibition race. With his good qualifying run, based on what she thought she understood, the signs for him were good.

And to his credit, he was grinning at Sam, however much he might have liked to be in his twin's place. Holding on to his nephew, he approached her. "I think Sam's a little bit excited."

"He is. Are you okay?"

"Sure. All part of the deal. Anyway, after yesterday…" They shared a glance of understanding. "How are you doing?"

"Fine. Okay, I shredded three tissues, just watching from the hauler."

"Wait till the race next Sunday. Better bring a whole box."

She pressed a hand to her stomach. "I have no idea how these women do it. Or why on earth you think this is fun."

Bart chuckled. "It's an acquired taste." He glanced down at the boy hopping from one foot to the other, craning for a glimpse of Will. "Though I'd say in his case it might be genetic."

Zoe shuddered. "Don't say that. It's bad enough, and Will's a grown man."

"What? He hasn't told you about the quarter-midget we found?"

Zoe gasped. "No. Tell me you're kidding."

The famed Branch twin mischief danced in his eyes. "I'm kidding."

She narrowed her own. "I don't know whether to believe you. Will wouldn't, surely, not without—"

Bart placed one hand on her arm. "Chill, Mama Bear. No, he wouldn't do that to you. Honest."

Her jitters eased but didn't disappear. She was grateful that Sam wasn't close enough to have heard, but that didn't mean he wouldn't be thrilled with the idea. Racing was in the air and a very real part of his life already. It was only a matter of time before the subject had to be dealt with.

And she wasn't remotely ready.

"Hey, I'm sorry. I just rained on your parade, didn't I? Don't listen to me. You know Will's smart mouth and mine get us into trouble all the time. Forget what I said. This is a really happy time for all of you. Don't let me spoil it."

"There he is!" Sam shouted. "Mom, there's Dad." He turned to her, face alight. "Can we go see him?"

"We'd better not—"

"Of course you can," Bart interrupted, grabbing her hand and gripping Sam's shoulder. "He'll want you there. Follow me."

Zoe had little choice, and falling in behind Bart's broad shoulders, she soon found herself ten feet away from where Will stood, holding the pole flag and a trophy while cameras snapped like crazy.

Then he spotted them and waved them over.

"Wow, Mom, he wants us."

No, she tried to mouth to Will. *It's not a good idea.*

But he was having none of it.

"Go, Zoe," Bart said.

"But the publicity…" And they weren't a family, not really. "Sam can go, but not—"

Bart's big hand landed in the middle of her back, and she found herself launched forward, ready or not.

Will moved to meet them, lifting Sam in one arm and holding her with the other. "Smile, sweetheart. This is all your doing."

Startled, she glanced at him. "What do you mean?"

"Thank you for last night. Thank you for the second chance. And thank you for wearing my locket." Then he bent and kissed her, and a barrage of camera flashes lit up the night.

"But—" There was so much left unresolved between them, yet when she saw Sam hugging his father and lifting his arms in triumph, yelling into the mike, "My dad rocks!"

What was she to do but let them both enjoy it?

THE FOLLOWING DAYS were a whirl. Cocktail parties, sponsor meetings, fan events… Will was in constant motion. As Zoe tried to get her footing in the midst of this carnival that was Speedweek, she found herself, in the odd quiet moment, trying to picture how she would ever fit in. How she and Will could possibly form a family that could survive his racing.

Not that he'd asked her to. The topic of marriage had been tabled, and every day her doubts increased as she realized just what the demands on Will were. How many people depended on him to give driving his all. For every person on the team in attendance at the track, there were many more back at the shop, all of whose families and livelihoods depended on the team winning races.

Yet day after day, Will got up very early and returned extremely late—and slept on the sofa, where his tall frame couldn't possibly be comfortable.

She did what she could to make things easy on him, even if he refused to take his bed back. She handled his laundry, took over the cooking from Mike and conspired to pack the calories and protein to bolster Will's strength. Daytona was as much an endurance contest for the drivers as it was a big party for the fans. It was stock car racing's Super Bowl, with all the attendant hoopla. Even Sam, with his endless energy, was dragging.

"Are you okay, Zoe?" Patsy Grosso asked at a barbecue she and Sam were attending, with Will due to arrive soon.

"Oh, yes, of course." She had no missing child, no piece of her heart lost as Patsy did. "I'm sorry. Just woolgathering."

"You're worn out, aren't you? Daytona's pretty overwhelming the first time, but don't worry. You'll learn to pace yourself next time."

Next time. Sam was really close, so she lowered her voice. "I doubt there'll be a next time."

Patsy's kind eyes softened. "Of course there will. That man isn't just crazy about his boy, you know. Everyone's noticed."

"Noticed what?"

"How his eyes follow you when you're not looking."

"Oh, Patsy, I don't think it's good for him for us to be here." She sniffed back tears. Turned her body a little so Sam wouldn't see her. "I'm sorry. You must think I'm a total wimp. I mean, look at you. You make it look easy."

"Hardly," Patsy scoffed. "There is nothing easy about this life, for any of us."

"So why do you do it?"

Patsy smiled. "I see how you look at him, too, you know. We do it for the same reason. Because we love them."

She did love Will, she was forced to admit, if only to herself. But that wasn't the point. "He has a lot on his shoulders, and he gets more nervous by the day. So much is on the line, and I think that maybe Sam and I should just…go. Now. So Will can focus only on racing."

"Oh, sweetie, that's your own nerves talking." Patsy patted her arm. "I completely understand. Dean turned into a bear before every race. Kent did it differently, at least until he found Tanya—he went looking for a party. I'm so glad she has to deal with his pre-race jitters now." She shook her head. "I sound like a terrible mother, don't I?"

"You sound like the gold standard of racing wives and mothers. That's what Maeve calls you."

Patsy's cheeks took on color. "Bless Maeve. She's sure had a rough time of it."

"So have you—still *are,* for that matter. I'm sorry for what's going on. And I probably should be keeping my mouth shut. It would make me crazy, not knowing."

Patsy's eyes went soft and haunted. She tapped her heart. "In here, I always felt…" She shook her head. "Everyone told me to give up on my baby, to focus on the family I had left. I did my best, and I didn't let myself think about her all the time, but…I never gave up hope. Even now, when I've missed her whole life—"

Tears welled, and Zoe felt horrible. "Patsy, I'm really sorry I brought it up."

"No." Patsy wiped at the tears with her finger. "Don't be sorry. However much pain it brings back, I have missed talking about my Gina. No one wants to talk about her, but she lived. She was real, and she's still real to me, even if—" Her voice faltered. "Even if this is all a terrible lie, this blogger."

She fell silent for a moment. "Even after all this time, having one minute, one single second to touch her face, to see the woman my baby might have become…" She faced Zoe. "It would be precious, so precious to me. As having Sam in his life now is to Will. Don't leave him, honey, not now. I promise you that knowing you're behind him is ten times more crucial to Will than any distraction you think you're presenting."

Zoe glanced around for Sam, relieved that he'd moved off. "I don't know what to do."

"Listen to your heart, sweetie. Don't let your fears win."

Just then, she saw Sam returning with Will in tow. "I don't know if I can," she answered, pasting on a smile. "But I'll try." Then she hugged Patsy hard. "I'll pray for you to find her. Please let me know if there's anything I can do to help."

Patsy returned the hug. "Thank you. I will. And you do the same." She patted Zoe's arm and left.

Zoe waited where she was. And found Will's heated eyes locked on hers.

"Here he is, Mom. Want some barbecue, Dad? I can get you some." He was hovering more than before. Always eager to be wherever Will was, he seemed almost clingy tonight, more than ever in need of his father's attention.

He would be beside himself if they left before the race. But were they taking precious time away from Will's preparation?

What was the right thing to do for both of them?

"That'd be great, son. You sure you can handle a full plate?"

Sam rolled his eyes. "Dad, I'm almost ten."

Will gave him a mock-punch on the shoulder. "Practically grown. But hold on, have you eaten?" he asked Zoe.

Excitement shimmered around him. It was like standing next to the sun. "What is it?"

"Answer me first. Are you hungry?"

"Not really."

"Go ahead, Sam," he said. "I'll work on your mom."

"Sure, Dad!" Sam was off like a shot.

Will was staring at her, eating her up with his eyes.

"What? What's going on?"

"My knucklehead brother gets it right, now and again."

"Oh?"

"He's going to ask Sam to stay with him tonight."

"Why?" She frowned. "I don't know if Sam will want to be away from you."

Will snorted. "Of course he will. Bart lets him get away with murder."

"But why would Bart want to do that on the night before a big race?"

"Because he's not always a total flea brain." Will's eyebrows lifted, his face a huge grin. "Seems he thought Sam's mama might want to stay with me."

Making love with Will…a thrill shivered through her.

Those hands, those lips…that hard, muscled body…

"Cat got your tongue?" His tone was teasing, but she saw a flicker of uncertainty in his gaze.

In that moment she realized that she couldn't leave him at such a critical point in his life. She'd been foolish to think so. And he was right, Sam loved being with Bart, too.

Abandoning the notion that she had to go freed the restraints she'd kept on herself, and she was flooded with desire. She smiled slowly. Wickedly. "Your brother may have just become my favorite person."

"Stop that."

"What?" she asked innocently.

"Don't look at me that way. We're surrounded by people."

"And isn't it a pity?" Could this be her, having fun, teasing?

"You're killing me, babe." Will all but dragged her around the front of the motor home, into the shadows, where he proceeded to kiss her until she swore her ears were ringing. Or maybe it was angels trumpeting.

Or Fate laughing at her.

Then someone from the party rounded the corner. "I think I saw them go— Uh-oh. Um, let's check at the back, Sam," said the voice that was unmistakably Bart.

Zoe straightened quickly, brushed at her hair.

Will grabbed her and kissed her again.

"Will!"

"He's with Bart. He'll be fine."

They heard other voices then. Will leaned his forehead against hers and sighed. "Why can't we be on the moon? Or at least not in the infield?"

"Why? It's only us and several thousand of your closest friends." She smiled at him.

He pinched the end of her nose lightly. "Come on, vixen. You're enjoying this too much. Let's go find our child and get this evening over with." But he was grinning back as he complained.

Zoe laughed and followed him.

IT WASN'T QUITE SO SIMPLE as waving Sam goodbye, Will discovered. First there was the packing, the deciding how much Sam would need. Will was baffled by how much the boy chose to take over there with him when he'd be back here in several hours, but Will didn't argue with him. All he could think about was Zoe. Sharing that big bed in the back of the motor home, for the first time ever, with someone who mattered.

She mattered. Zoe. Sam, too. As soon as Daytona was over, he was putting the full-court press on her to find a way for them to be together full-time. Sandra had even asked if Zoe might be interested in a job, and it had set Will to thinking. If Zoe was intent on earning her own way, there could be possibilities in the traveling road show that was NASCAR. He could find a tutor for Sam, or they could....

He was getting ahead of himself, he knew that. But he didn't know how he could just put them on a plane tomorrow night and not know how long it might be before they were together again.

"Penny for your thoughts," Zoe asked as they strolled to his motor home, one away from Bart's. Sam and Bart were engrossed in a video game, one that might take them hours to finish.

Thank you, bro. His mom and Chuck had offered to take Sam for the night, but he'd been pretty sure Sam wouldn't like leaving the infield the night before the big race, however much he adored Maeve and Chuck. He owed Bart, big-time.

"It's funny how kids stay with you, even when you're not with them," he said. "It's not so easy to just turn them off, is it?"

She shook her head. "Not at all."

"But you're okay with letting him stay over?" He couldn't believe he was actually offering to go reclaim Sam and give up this night together.

She shrugged. "Not completely, but only because I've been away from him so seldom. I know he'll be fine with Bart, well, as fine as any child can be in the care of his very indulgent bachelor uncle."

They both smiled. "Bart would take a bullet for him."

"I know." She turned to him. Laid her palm on his cheek. "He's very lucky to have become part of your family. I'm so happy for him."

Her words sent a quiet pride through him. He wanted to tell her that she was a part of them, too, that he wanted to bind her even closer.

But that might start an argument, and he didn't want to fight with Zoe tonight. Furthest thing from it. In the darkness, he drew her against the side of his motor home, unable to wait to hold her until they got inside. "Oh, love," he said as he tightened his arms around her. "I'm so glad you're here."

She stiffened slightly. "We're not a distraction?"

He had to chuckle. "You're one hell of a distraction, honey—but in the best of ways."

She gripped him. "I want you safe tomorrow, Will. I know winning's important, but you be careful out there, promise me?"

Her fervor made his heart sing. He was becoming important to her, too. The knowledge nearly had him bringing up the proposal he wasn't sure she was ready for yet.

She took the matter out of his hands. Or into her hands, more to the point. Caresses, heated kisses, slow strokes over his chest—this was a lot like the Zoe of a recent memorable night.

Only she wasn't drunk this time.

And he didn't have to be chivalrous.

"Zoe," he groaned, and swept her up in his arms, somehow managing to get both of them up the steps and inside before she stripped off his shirt and he lost his mind.

Soon, however, both of them were ensconced in their own private world of rough urgency and tender sighs, of piercing emotion and ragged desire. The night flared hot, and their hearts soared. The man and the woman formed from all that had happened to a long-ago boy and girl opened their hearts to one another and, through the magic of touch and taste and sweet caresses, found their way back to the place that was theirs alone.

And in the deepest dark of night, no one saw the small figure creep quietly out of a motor home, his backpack clutched in two small hands.

Leaving behind him a note in careful block print.

CHAPTER SEVENTEEN

WILL KNEW they needed to get up and retrieve Sam pretty soon, but Zoe was in his bed, soft and sweet, and he couldn't keep his hands off her. He was well on his way to waking her up in the most delicious way he could imagine and—

Loud knocks on his door. "Will! Open up, damn it."

Bart. And he didn't sound happy.

Will leaped from the bed and yanked on jeans. Zoe grabbed a robe and wasn't far behind him as he opened the door.

"What's wrong? Where's Sam?"

Bart glanced from one to the next. "I've already called security."

Zoe gasped. Will pulled her into his side. "What happened?"

"He's gone. I don't know how he got out without waking me up. I am so damn sorry. I didn't think I was sleeping that soundly."

Zoe had gone pale. "Why? Why would he go? Could someone have grabbed him?"

Bart shook his head. "I wouldn't have slept through that." He proffered a sheet of paper torn from a note pad. "He left this."

Mom
I don't want to leave. I heard you tell Mrs. Grosso we had to go. Dad needs us to stay, and I know you won't

leave without me. He'll win Daytona and everything will be fine, you'll see.

Don't be mad. I'll find you after Dad wins.

Love, Sam

Zoe's hand went to her mouth. "Where is he? Oh dear heaven, what have I done?" She pulled away from him.

"It's going to be all right, sweetheart. We'll find him, I promise."

"I didn't think he heard," she said brokenly.

"Why were you leaving?" He fought the sharp sense of betrayal. When she started to answer, he shook his head. "Never mind. I know. You've made it very clear how you feel about racing." He turned away, heart heavy with the knowledge that she still had no faith in him. That she was no closer to accepting the life they could make.

"I have to go look for him. I should never have let him out of my sight."

"You stay here. I'll go." Will traded glances with Bart, who was looking at him with sympathy. "What are the security guys doing?"

"They want a picture, if you have one. Listen, I'm really sorry—"

"It's not your fault."

"It's mine," Zoe said. But her look said that she blamed Will, too.

"Zoe, I'll find him. I swear it."

"There are thousands of people out there. Some of them have been drinking all night. He doesn't know his way around. He could get lost, he could get run over by some fool—" She pressed her lips together and visibly pulled herself straight. "You have a lot to do today, both of you. I'll take care of it." Her voice was cold as the grave.

Will's jaw dropped. "Are you insane? You think any of this is as important to me as my child? What the hell kind of opinion do you have of me, Zoe?" But he knew. *You left me once,* she might as well be saying. Fury rode him hard, but fury did Sam no good.

He wheeled and went to the album that was always with him, Zoe's Christmas present. Though he hated to lose a single scrap of it, he removed the most recent photo of Sam and handed it to Bart. "Here. Will you meet with security? I'm going looking." He strode to his bedroom to dress quickly.

As he left the bedroom, Zoe slipped past him. "What are you doing?" he asked her.

"If you think I'm just sitting on my hands while my baby is out there alone—"

"We can go together. You don't know your way around."

"I'm a big girl," she snapped. "I'll do fine on my own."

"Of course," he said bitterly. "That's how you prefer it." He brushed past his twin, then paused. "Call Mom and Chuck, okay? I've got my cell if anything comes up."

Bart nodded soberly. "Want me to call Taney for you? Explain about whatever appointments you're missing?"

Will shook his head. "You get on with your day as planned. I'll call him and Kylie. They'll have to understand."

"You're kidding, right? I'm going to go do meet-and-greets when my nephew is lost?"

"One of us should stay out of hot water. Your ride isn't much more secure than mine."

"They'll have to understand, isn't that what you said? Family, bro. Sam is family. And I'm damn sorry this happened. I thought I was giving you a great night."

Will glanced back at the woman who'd become a stranger once again. "You did. Maybe once Sam's back, she'll remember that."

IN THE END, though Zoe had been determined to scour every last inch of ground herself, she'd had to bow to the wisdom of the experts, who insisted that someone Sam knew had to be stationed at each place that was familiar to him. Will's team had the garage and hauler staked out; Maeve was holding down the fort in Bart's motor home. Zoe was advised to remain in the place that was most like home to Sam: Will's motor home.

She paced. She phoned every person she could think of. She badgered the track security chief without mercy.

Finally, Kylie was appointed to babysit her.

"You don't have to stay here."

"I don't mind. I'd be going insane in your place."

"Where's Ryan?" Zoe finally thought to ask.

"With my husband, talking to all the kids he and Sam have played with."

"Oh, they shouldn't be—"

"Zoe." Kylie's tone was firm. "This is NASCAR. We're a family. There's not a driver, a crew member, a concession stand worker, a wife or a driver's kid who isn't looking for Sam. He'll turn up. We take care of each other."

"I don't understand." Zoe fought tears for the hundredth time. "Why would they?"

"You're one of us now. And people care about Will and Bart. Bart is beating himself up pretty badly, by the way. Even so, he looks a hundred times better than Will."

"What do you mean?"

"I saw him on the way over here. He's aged ten years, I swear. He just about took my head off when I reminded—" Abruptly she stopped.

"Reminded him about what?"

"Nothing."

"Kylie, tell me. What is he missing?" Though Zoe had a hard time caring about a sponsor's needs right now.

"The drivers' meeting started ten minutes ago."

"That's important, right?"

"Very. If Will misses the meeting, he loses the pole. Goes

to the back of the field, and it's really hard to win from there."

Zoe thought about how excited Will had been a few days ago, brandishing the pole flag. Having his picture taken with the special trophy. Insisting on Sam and her being in the picture.

"I have to call him. Tell him to go on. He can't miss this."

"It won't do any good. I'm not the only person urging him to go. He's like a man possessed searching for his son."

Zoe felt sick. Guilt crowded into the worry that had consumed her. She'd been so sure Will would be the one to hurt Sam.

She'd never dreamed she'd hurt Sam far worse. And now she was dealing a blow to Will's career, too.

Because of her distrust.

How can I prove anything to you if you don't give me a chance?

I'm a big girl, she'd snapped at him. *I'll do fine on my own.*

Of course. That's how you prefer it.

She thought about how it felt to lie in his arms. Saw her little boy's glow when he was with his beloved dad. Remembered Will with tears in his eyes over pictures of the childhood he'd missed.

Don't be mad. I'll find you after Dad wins.

But Will wouldn't win now.

And it was all her fault.

She picked up her cell and dialed Will's number.

"Any news?" He sounded completely exhausted.

"No."

"Why are you calling?" So cold. Not the Will she knew.

"Go to the drivers' meeting, Will. Please." She inhaled deeply and prayed she was right. "Sam said he'd find us after the race. He's a smart little boy."

"Are you nuts? Anything could happen to him. I'm not stopping until—wait."

"What?" A clutch in her heart.

"Thank you, God." He heaved a huge sigh. "He's here."

"What did you say?"

"I see him. I'm going to him now. I'll bring him to you."

"Will, wait! Where are you?"

"At my hauler. Sam—"

Zoe could hear her child's voice just as the phone clattered and she was cut off. "Will found him." She didn't wait for Kylie but raced out the door.

AT LAST WILL UNDERSTOOD why his mother yelled at him when she was most worried. "Where have you been?"

"We found him under the hauler," Mike said. "Behind one set of wheels."

"What on earth were you thinking?" Will dropped to his knees and crushed Sam to him.

"Dad, you're supposed to be in the drivers' meeting."

Torn by the conflicting desires to never let go of his son and to shake him senseless, it took a second for Sam's words to penetrate. "What?"

"You shouldn't be here. You can't miss the drivers' meeting or you'll lose the pole."

Now Will couldn't decide whether to laugh or cry or yell. "You think I'd go to a meeting when you're missing?" Then anger took over. "You could have been hurt. Someone could have picked you up. We were going out of our minds worrying about you."

"I left a note," Sam said in a small voice. "I said I'd find you after you won."

"Why did you go? Why didn't you talk to us? You scared us half to death. Hundreds of people have been looking for you. Your mother is frightened out of her mind."

Sam's eyes were wet. "I heard her tell Mrs. Grosso we had to leave. That we're a distraction for you. She doesn't think we can be a family, and I couldn't let her make us go. You need us, don't you, Dad?"

Will crushed him close again. "You bet I do." Motion behind Sam had him looking up.

Zoe stood there, stricken, tears spilling down her cheeks. Will locked eyes with hers. "I love you. I love both of you. I want us to be a family. I think we can make it work." She looked so devastated that he continued, "But your mom hasn't been so lucky as you, having family to trust. She's been alone a long time, and it's harder for her to believe."

Sam turned. "We can, Mom. Please…please try."

"Oh, honey." She gathered him in. Bent over him, shoulders shaking.

"I'm sorry, Mom. I didn't know how to convince you."

Zoe kissed his head. Looked up at Will. "Is it too late? If you went now, would they—"

Will shook his head. She seemed crestfallen. "I am so sorry, Will, I never meant to cost you a race."

"If you think a race is more important than our child's safety, you're wrong."

He could see it sinking in with her, at last. Watched the knowledge bloom in her eyes that he'd chosen family over racing. "Believe me now?" he asked softly, only for her ears.

"I'm so sorry, Will. So sorry my lack of faith cost you dearly."

He rose. "But do you?"

She nodded, a tremulous smile on her lips. "I do."

"Thank God." He folded her into him, pressed a kiss to her hair, rocking her slowly. Savoring how she went soft against him.

"You should hate me." Sam's shoulders rounded in despair.

Will drew back but clasped Zoe's hand, then knelt down before Sam. "I could never hate you, son. You need some work on thinking through the consequences of your decisions, and we will be talking about punishment for this escapade, but I actually admire what you did."

Sam's head rose swiftly. "You do?"

"Not how you did it, don't get confused. But that you were standing up for something you believed in very strongly. You were trying to help me out by keeping your mom here, and I appreciate that. We'll be discussing different ways to achieve that goal, but I have to give you credit that you meant well."

Sam's lower lip trembled. "So…you still love me?"

"More than ever." He stood and brushed the tears from Zoe's cheek. "And I love your mother."

Her gaze held his, and something inside him settled.

"So what happens now, Dad?"

Will made promises to her without words, and her smile said she understood. He dragged his attention away and turned to Sam. "Well, first we all get some food and maybe a quick nap. Then I go race as hard as I can."

"What do I do?"

"You cheer as hard as you ever have in your life 'cause I'll hear it. I'll know you're with me on the track."

"Mom, too. Right, Mom?"

She brushed his hair. "You better believe it."

"I'd like you to watch from my pit box, you and your mom. Think you can handle it?"

Sam's eyes went wide as saucers. "Yeah!" Quickly, though, he slanted a look at Zoe. "Would that be okay, Mom?"

Will saw her smother a smile and did so himself. The boy was a fast learner.

"That would be wonderful. If Dad's positive we won't be a distraction."

He resisted the urge to roll his eyes. "The boy's a quick study," he leaned over and whispered to her. "But his mother is a wee bit stubborn."

"Sorry. Yes, we'd love to."

"I still think you're gonna win, Dad."

"From your mouth to God's ear, as my granny used to say." He drew them both close and held on tight. "But wherever I finish on the track, I'm already a winner if I have you two." He looked at Zoe. "Do I?"

She nodded and rose to kiss him. "You do. We'll figure it all out."

Will wasted not one second sealing the deal.

WILL DID INDEED race his heart out. He didn't win, but he pulled off a top-five finish, little short of a miracle. Bart came in two spots behind him. Crucial points to begin the season.

Back in Dallas a week later, Zoe looked around her at the nearly bare apartment. Only a few more boxes to pack. Sandra had offered her an entry-level job with Motor Media Group, and Zoe was seriously considering it. Kylie had recommended a private school where other drivers' kids went, one that made allowances for racing schedules, assigning work to take with them so that the students had the option to travel with their families at least part of the time.

They were moving into Will's condo in Charlotte, but since Will had promised Sam a dog, they wouldn't be staying long before looking for a house with a yard.

And planning a wedding. Zoe's stomach fluttered at the thought of being Mrs. Will Branch after all these years. Steps were in place to change Sam's name legally, and her child was over the moon.

Life was looking bright. There was only one shadow.

She missed Will desperately. He was on the West Coast, and they'd agreed it didn't make sense for him to come back between California and Las Vegas.

Her heart hadn't gotten the message.

But she'd agreed to give this life a fair shot, and time apart was part of the deal. Sam was in school, finishing up the six weeks, then the movers would come and they'd be leaving Texas for North Carolina.

A knock at the door startled her from her thoughts. Probably Maeve, who'd been a godsend, helping her pack, offering to store things at the family home she and Chuck had decided would be their primary residence.

Happy for the company, she opened the door. "Hi, Maeve—" Surprise stopped her cold.

"Hey, gorgeous." Will stood there, violets in hand, grinning.

"What are you doing here?"

He snagged her around the waist, danced her inside. "Aren't you going to congratulate me for winning California?"

"I already di—" Her words were lost in his heated kiss. She dropped the blouse she'd been folding.

Will locked the door. Picked her up without breaking the kiss and started for the bedroom.

Thrilled, Zoe wrapped her legs around his waist, started laughing. "Hello to you, too."

"Sam's at school, right?" His eyes sparkled.

"Yes, but what are you—"

He covered her mouth again.

Zoe sighed. Grabbed on tight.

He spilled her to the mattress, set the flowers on the bedside table. Yanked his shirt over his head in one swift move. "I missed you. I needed to be with my family."

"But you look exhausted."

His smile was warm and wicked. "Oh, I'm not dead yet."

She smiled back. "I'm glad you're here. I was just thinking how badly I wanted to see you."

"Great minds…" He tapped his temple. "Now if I have it right, Sam won't be home for close to two hours."

"Mmm-hmm." She nodded. "Plenty of time. You can even get a nap."

His look dripped pity. "Oh, baby…you have forgotten entirely too much if you think that. Two hours will barely get us started on what I've been thinking about doing to you." He dropped to the bed on top of her, startling a squeal. "Allow me to refresh your memory."

But even as she giggled, she had to take a minute and study his beloved features, tracing his jaw. "I am so happy to see you."

"Even though I'm turning your life inside out?" His tone was teasing, but his expression was absolutely serious.

"To the contrary…at last, I feel like I'm coming home."

"We are going to make a home, sweetheart. A real family, the forever kind."

For a second, she lost her nerve. "What if we can't?" Forever was foreign to her experience.

He caressed her face, pressed a soft kiss to her lips. "I believe in us, Zoe—you, me and Sam. Maybe a few more down the road," he added, and something inside her warmed at the notion of having more children with him. "It'll take work, yes, from all of us," he acknowledged. "But I know we can do it."

"I believe you." Zoe looked at him, this man she'd loved for so long and realized that she really did. That she trusted him with her whole heart. That she wasn't afraid anymore. "I love you, Will."

At her words, he sobered. "I love you, too, sweetheart. More than you can imagine." He buried his face in her hair and held her for a precious moment.

Then he playfully rolled her over on top of him. "Watch

out, world," he whispered, as his mouth cruised over her skin and made her shiver.

That cocky Will Branch grin of old emerged, eliciting a smile in return. "Better put your money on the Branches," he said, his eyes locking with hers.

"'Cause we are going for the win."

* * * * *

*For more thrill-a-minute romances set against
the exciting backdrop of the NASCAR world, don't miss
CHECKERED FLAG by Abby Gaines*

*Available in March
For a sneak peek, just turn the page!*

CHAD'S WHOLE LIFE HAD BEEN out of whack since he'd met Brianna, and that had to stop. Now was a good time. "How do we go about finding closure?"

"I think," she said, "we discuss how we feel about what went wrong."

"Uh-huh. You go first," he said encouragingly, and dug into his stew.

She put down her knife and fork. "You said you loved me."

Chad choked on a piece of carrot, and just about had it coming out his nose. Brianna packed a mighty punch when she chose to. "Can't we start somewhere else?" he said, indignant, when he'd finished coughing.

"Was it a lie?" Her brown gaze was clear, searching.

Dammit, she wasn't going to drop it. He wiped his mouth with his napkin, stalling for time. The easiest thing would be to say he'd gotten carried away, mistaken infatuation, or lust, for love. He willed himself to take the easy way out.

"It wasn't a lie," he said. For Pete's sake, what happened to his willpower when she was around?

She nodded slowly. "Then…?"

That was the one-word, sixty-four-thousand-dollar question.

"You said the same thing," he reminded her.

Brianna rubbed her arms, as if she was cold. "I wasn't lying, either."

A part of Chad wanted to whoop for joy. But it wasn't the mature, together part of him, which he relied on to get through life.

"I didn't realize then that love is about more than talking about your feelings," she said. "Love is something you do. Or not."

"I did love you," he said. "It wasn't just words." If he could just forget the need to prove himself, this would be a lot easier.

She twirled the stem of her wineglass between her fingers; the red liquid swayed and sloshed. "I don't think a guy who loved his wife would let her leave so easily."

"You mean, it was all my fault?"

"Not all," she said. Unconvincingly.

"Maybe a woman who loved her husband wouldn't give up on him just because he didn't automatically want her in every part of his life." He took a swig of his own wine. "Maybe she'd take a chance they could work things out."

Her eyes widened, as if she'd never considered the possibility. Whereas Chad had second-guessed that morning so many times....

"I couldn't," she said. "I've never mattered to anyone, Chad." Brianna pressed her fingertips onto the edge of the table. "Are you surprised I didn't want more from my marriage?"

He dodged a stab of guilt. "Are you surprised I wasn't ready to share every breath I take with someone I'd known only three days?"

"Then why did you ask me to marry you?"

Their voices had risen, and people at the surrounding tables were staring. This was crazy, Chad thought. No wonder he hadn't gotten married before; it was like walking through a minefield in hobnail boots.

He took a deep breath. "You and I are two totally different people, and if we'd spent five minutes together in our normal environment, we would have realized that."

"You're right," she said. "Our marriage was all wrong."

"So—" ignoring the heaviness in his chest, he took his argument to its logical conclusion "—it's probably a good idea if we get that divorce started." *And stop talking about things that are only going to hurt us.*

"No rush," she said. Which, suddenly, was nowhere near enough information.

"You're not...seeing anyone?" Pressure built, as if his heart were being squeezed by a fist inside his chest. It was a natural possessiveness, Chad assured himself, a caveman instinct any red-blooded guy would feel toward his wife.

"I'm not seeing anyone." She paused. "I haven't seen anyone."

The grip on his heart loosened, and his blood resumed pumping.

The conversation felt one-sided. "Aren't you going to ask if I'm seeing someone?" he asked.

"I'm not sure I want to know."

REQUEST YOUR FREE BOOKS!
2 FREE NOVELS PLUS 2 FREE GIFTS!

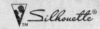

SPECIAL EDITION®
Life, Love and Family!

YES! Please send me 2 FREE Silhouette Special Edition® novels and my 2 FREE gifts (gifts are worth about $10). After receiving them, if I don't wish to receive any more books, I can return the shipping statement marked "cancel." If I don't cancel, I will receive 6 brand-new novels every month and be billed just $4.24 per book in the U.S. or $4.99 per book in Canada, plus 25¢ shipping and handling per book and applicable taxes, if any*. That's a savings of at least 15% off the cover price! I understand that accepting the 2 free books and gifts places me under no obligation to buy anything. I can always return a shipment and cancel at any time. Even if I never buy another book from Silhouette, the two free books and gifts are mine to keep forever.

235 SDN EEYU 335 SDN EEY6

Name	(PLEASE PRINT)	
Address		Apt. #
City	State/Prov.	Zip/Postal Code

Signature (if under 18, a parent or guardian must sign)

Mail to the **Silhouette Reader Service:**
IN U.S.A.: P.O. Box 1867, Buffalo, NY 14240-1867
IN CANADA: P.O. Box 609, Fort Erie, Ontario L2A 5X3

Not valid to current subscribers of Silhouette Special Edition books.

Want to try two free books from another line?
Call 1-800-873-8635 or visit www.morefreebooks.com.

* Terms and prices subject to change without notice. N.Y. residents add applicable sales tax. Canadian residents will be charged applicable provincial taxes and GST. Offer not valid in Quebec. This offer is limited to one order per household. All orders subject to approval. Credit or debit balances in a customer's account(s) may be offset by any other outstanding balance owed by or to the customer. Please allow 4 to 6 weeks for delivery. Offer available while quantities last.

Your Privacy: Silhouette is committed to protecting your privacy. Our Privacy Policy is available online at www.eHarlequin.com or upon request from the Reader Service. From time to time we make our lists of customers available to reputable third parties who may have a product or service of interest to you. If you would prefer we not share your name and address, please check here. ☐

SSE08R

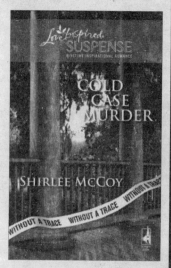